I0574189

# Don't Make Me

*A Bad Boy Mafia Romance*

## Made Men

### Renee Rose

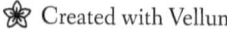 Created with Vellum

# Want FREE Renee Rose books?

*the Marine* and more. In addition to the free stories, you will also get bonus epilogues, special pricing, exclusive previews and news of new releases.

# Prologue

## Sicily

**C**arlo

Blood soaks my clothes—too much to show up at my great-uncle Junior's front entrance. I slip around to the back and tap the heavy wooden door. I hope Zia Maria doesn't answer, not that the old woman can't handle the shock. Sicilian women—at least those in *La Famiglia*—are as tough as the men.

The door cracks, and the muzzle of a Glock points through followed by my uncle's bushy white eyebrows.

"*Carlo.*" The door swings wide, and my uncle grabs me by the shirt and hauls me inside.

"Only some of it is mine." I can't get my damn ear to stop bleeding from the bullet that went through. The bullet that missed my skull by an inch.

"Get cleaned up before your aunt sees you." The old man propels me to the bathroom. "I'll bring you some clothes."

I strip, the metallic smell of blood filling my nostrils.

1

Ferdi's blood. Fucking Ferdi. I left him alive after I beat the truth out of him.

Who tries to kill their own cousin? Ferdi, apparently.

I won't. I didn't. Ferdi's soldier, though, is another story. I left a bullet in the middle of his forehead. Closing my eyes, I try to erase the sight.

I wash in the shower and dry off, barely managing to keep the continuous drip of blood from my ear from staining Zia Maria's towel.

My uncle comes in without knocking and drops some clothes on the counter. He gives me an up-and-down sweep of the eyes, probably checking for bullet holes. "Just the ear?"

"Yeah." I yank on the clothes.

"Who?" Junior hands me a washcloth and lifts his chin toward my still-bleeding ear.

"Ferdi."

My uncle's bushy eyebrows drew together. "Your *cousin* Ferdi? What happened?"

"Mario put a hit on me." I somehow keep the waver from my voice, unprepared for the sense of betrayal rocketing through my chest. *My own fucking brother.* My fucking brother ordered me killed.

Junior's face turns to stone, his eyes black and dangerous. It's an expression I've seen on my father's face countless times. The Sicilian war face. Calculating, deadly. "What happened? Wait, come out of the fucking bathroom. I'll get you a drink."

At the kitchen table, Junior pours both of us a glass of grappa, and we sit down.

"My dad named me Consiglieri. I think Mario thinks he might pick me to lead when he dies." My chest tightens at the thought of my father, so diminished from the cancer now.

"I see." My mom's uncle isn't part of the Romano business in Palermo, but his family has ties to them and runs their own network of semi-legal or illegal operations. He understands the dynamics. "What's your plan?"

That is the fucking problem. I don't have one.

Junior reads into the silence. "Are you going to tell your dad?"

I give my head a decisive shake. "Hell no. He's on his deathbed. It would kill him, and he would die broken-hearted."

"Let me ask you this, Carlo. Do you *want* to lead the family? I mean, how old are you? Twenty-three?"

"Yeah."

"I mean, I know you're smart, and I'm sure you're tough, but do you think the older guys are going to fall in line under you?"

I shrug. "I wasn't trying to steal the power from Mario... or any of them." Hell, I'm the *fifth* son, I never expected to be more than a capo. But as the youngest child, I have the special ability of reading people. Born from all that time observing from corners as a kid, I suppose. I see through bullshit, see into people. My father used that talent in the last few years, coming to me much more often than he did Mario or any of our other brothers.

We always were tight, me and my dad. I'm the baby

of the family, after all. My dad wasn't as much of a hard-ass with me as he was with my brothers; and more than that, my parents revered me as a special gift because I almost died during birth.

"Look, I don't even know if my father would have shaken up the structure. But obviously, Mario was worried. So now I'm in a bad place."

The soft pad of Zia Maria's slippers scuffing the floor signal her approach from down the hall.

"It's Carlo," Junior calls to her.

"Carlo?" The joy in my aunt's voice almost makes me tear up. *Cristo*. I'm going soft. Well, when your own brother wants you dead, it's nice to know someone in the family still cares.

I stand and embrace the tiny woman, accept her clucking over my ear. I don't try to stop her from pulling out all the food in the fridge and heating it up for a full meal. You can't keep an Italian woman from that generation from feeding her family.

When I finish eating and successfully ward off Maria's pressure for seconds, she sits down with us.

"Mamma." Junior covers his wife's gnarled hand. "Carlo's in a pinch. His brother wants him dead because he's worried about his stealing power when their father dies."

I didn't expect Junior to tell Maria. Usually, the women are left out of business discussions—no one wants to incriminate the innocent. But this is a family issue, and right now I need help from my family.

Zia Maria covers her mouth with her hand, but when

she removes it, she already has a sharp look in her eye. She taps the table with her bony fingers. "Send him to my nephew Alberto, in New Jersey. Just until this all blows over. He could use a smart young man like our Carlo. He'll take good care of our boy."

I swallow the lump in my throat. I'd be away when my dad dies. Miss saying goodbye. And he wouldn't know where I've gone. But there is no way around it.

I draw a breath. *New Jersey.* Well, it sounds better than any plan I've come up with. "Okay." I nod. "That sounds good. Thank you."

# Chapter One

*New Jersey*
*Four Years Later*

**S**ummer

I grip the pole and extend one leg up into a perfect split. A lifetime of ballet lessons is finally paying off. Heh. Well, it's not like I can perform for real anymore, not since my injury.

I consider stripping at The Candy Store to be a form of sex therapy. That's how I framed it to my best friend, Maggie, anyway.

I don't strip for the money, and it sure as hell isn't to meet nice guys. But I like the sense of power it gives me. Or is it the objectification? Either way, each time I take the stage and twirl around the pole, it repairs a small piece of my shattered sexual confidence.

I have my asswipe ex-boyfriend John to thank for my new career. Every night I work, I feed off the lust in the men's eyes and send a psychic f-you to the guy who found me so unappealing. He barely managed to have sex with me once a month. When I found out he was cheating on me with multiple women—sometimes three different women in a week—I was ready to give up men altogether. But this is better.

So long as my father never finds out. Because Alberto LaTorre, don of the LaTorre Crime Family, would never recover from learning his spoiled *principessa* is taking her clothes off for money. He has some very old school Catholic ideas about women—they're either whores or the blessed Virgin herself, and nothing in between exists. And, obviously, he wants me firmly in the blessed virgin category.

I pull off my short plaid Catholic school girl skirt to the applause of the crowd. The white blouse is already off, leaving me in nothing but a bikini top and lacey white G-string. I crawl forward on the stage and accept a five-dollar bill between my tits, giving the man who offered it a nibble on his earlobe as I murmur "Thanks."

Standing to twirl around the pole again, I grip it and flip myself upside down with my legs in a forward split. Rotating my legs, I open them to a center split, then wrap both ankles around the pole and slide down to land on my back with my knees bent up and spread wide.

In my periphery, I see a couple guys enter through the door. Maybe it's the well-tailored suit that makes me look twice. Maybe it's just my instincts kicking into gear, but when I glance through the low-lit club at the faces of the men, I go cold.

*Carlo.*

My father's right-hand man. My drool-worthy, sexy Sicilian foster-brother of sorts, walking in like he owns the place. I recognize the face of the guy with him but don't know his name. One of Carlo's soldiers.

I spin to hide my face, praying he didn't see me. He'll probably head straight up to the VIP section for private dances. He certainly has the money and seems like the type who prefers that. Hopefully he won't even give the stage the time of day. Thank heavens no one around here will object to the sight of my ass instead of my face. I put my two hands on the upstage wall and roll my hips and head in concentric circles, letting my thick brown hair fall down my back. I wonder if I could just stay back there, pin to the wall until my set is over. Two more numbers, and I'll be off the stage, and then I'll tell my boss I'm not feeling well and split.

But already some young frat boys are hollering to me, waving their five-dollar bills in the air for me to come over. I pretend not to see them.

"Hey, over here," one of them calls. "What? Our money's not good enough for you?"

*"Milan."* My boss, Sam, grunts my stage name, jerking his head toward the guy. I toss my head around as I strut toward him, letting my hair fall over my face. Crouching down, I pull out the waistband of my G-string for his offering.

With my back to the audience, I go back to the pole and wrap one leg around it, humping the stainless steel. Going for another high kick, I slip and stumble back. It turns out sweaty palms present a serious impediment to pole dancers. To recover, I strut around the perimeter of the stage, trying to keep my hair over my face.

I don't look at Carlo. He climbed the stairs into the VIP section, but he's sitting at the balcony, looking down. It's probably just my imagination that he's staring straight at me. When I round the corner, I dart a glance in his direction.

Shit.

We lock gazes, and my stomach twists.

Carlo's lips flatten. Surging to his feet, he jogs down the stairs and stalks toward the stage. Jimmy, The Candy Store's ex-marine bouncer, flexes his muscles and steps forward.

I dart toward the stairs to intercept. As the daughter of Jersey's largest crime family don, I probably know even less than your average American about the workings of the mob, but there is one thing I understand: Family men don't take shit from anyone. Like any apex predator, they're dangerous when provoked.

"It's okay, Jimmy," I say breathlessly as I navigate the stage steps in my heels.

"Milan, what the hell are you doing?" Sam calls from the other side of the stage.

I send an apologetic glance at him and try to push past Jimmy, who put his body between mine and Carlo's. He extends an arm to hold me back.

"What do you want?" he demands of Carlo.

Carlo ignores him and lifts his chin at me. He doesn't need to speak. I know he can only have one agenda--to haul me out of there as fast as possible, before anyone else sees my scantily-clad body.

"It's okay, Jimmy." I grip the bouncer's bulging bicep.

Carlo looks at the place where my hand connects with Jimmy's arm, and his lip curls into a snarl.

I snatch it away. "I'm going to leave with Carlo. I have to go."

"Is this guy giving you problems? You don't have to go anywhere with him."

The stupid bouncer's going to get himself killed. Why can't he leave it the hell alone? "No, no. You have it all wrong. He's family."

*With a capital F.*

"He's my ride, and I have to go now."

By this time, Sam's shoved another girl on stage. He makes it over to us, looking irate. "What in the hell is going on here?"

"I'm sorry, Sam. I have to quit. You can keep my last paycheck. I'll just get my stuff from the locker room." I say the last bit to Carlo who acknowledges it with an almost imperceptible nod.

Jimmy catches my arm. "Are you in some kind of trouble?" he asks in a low voice.

"No! I'm not. I'm really not. But I do have to go. I'm really sorry." I pull away and rush off toward the locker room, carrying my clothes from the stage. I throw on my plaid skirt and white blouse and grab my purse from the locker.

Carlo and his soldier wait in the hall. Carlo stands out from the rest of the men who frequent The Candy

Store. Tall, expensively-dressed and darkly handsome, he caught the attention of all the women working the place, but right now he's looking only at me, and he appears lethal. Something about seeing Carlo as such a badass makes my entire body vibrate—and not just from nerves. I scoot past them, not wanting a scene in The Candy Store, and head out the back door with my two body-guards—or in this case, prison guards—behind me.

"You drive my car back." Carlo hands his keys to his soldier. The guy disappears, afraid enough of my father to avoid looking my way. Carlo follows me to my car.

"Are you going to tell me what in the fuck is going on?" His sexy Italian accent sounds thicker when he's mad. His green eyes flash.

I shiver and shake my head.

"No?" He cups my chin. Despite the hard lines and the anger on his face, his touch is gentle. "What were you doing in there? You can't possibly need the money." He gives me a questioning look.

"No, it's not that. I like dancing, okay?"

"Dancing?" He snorts. "I've seen you dance. You have more talent than every stripper in Jersey combined. That's not dancing. Give me the damn keys."

I search in my purse and produce them. "Are you going to tell my dad?"

He snatches the keyring from my hand. "Of course, I'm going to tell him. I'm going to drive you to his house right now, so he can straighten you out."

The thought of my father's reaction brings on a wave of panic. It's not that I'm afraid of him. It's what this would do to him. I'm his little princess. His perfect girl—the ballerina, the straight-A dance major whose parents hoped would someday marry a doctor or lawyer and be as straight-laced and square as they are marginal. I don't want to ruin my parents' little fantasy.

I block Carlo when he reaches to open the car door, getting a whiff of his cologne and, underneath it, his decidedly masculine scent. He towers over me, his hard-muscled body so close heat registers along my skin. "Don't tell him."

\* \* \*

*Carlo*

*Gesù*, if it wasn't so wrong, seeing Summer LaTorre on that stage would've been a wet dream come true. Her legs look impossibly long under the miniscule skirt, her breasts lush and ripe, pushed up by the tiny bikini top under her white blouse. This can't be the same princess I sit across from on Sunday meals at her father's house.

She grips my shirt, her beautiful copper-flecked eyes bright with tears. "You can't tell him. Please don't tell him."

If she had any idea how much her tearful begging turns me on, she'd run back for the protection of that jackass bouncer in a heartbeat. Or she should, anyway.

I force myself to ignore my growing hard-on. Her skimpy outfit doesn't help matters. But then, I've always had a difficult time keeping my thoughts pure when it comes to Summer LaTorre. *Gesù*, when I saw her thrashing her hips around up on that stage...

But turned on or not, the fact that the don's daughter is taking her clothes off for money concerns me. I suspect the reason behind it is even more unsettling than catching her in the act.

I cover her fists with my hands, resisting the urge to bring one to my lips to kiss. "Summer, you know where my loyalty lies. I can't keep this from him."

"Please, Carlo, you have to."

Damn, she's cute when she turns those puppy dog eyes on me. But no, I can't let this go. "Listen, doll, what you were doing in there" —I jerk my thumb toward the strip club— "isn't right. You need someone to straighten you the fuck out."

Summer blinks rapidly.

"You've been a hot mess ever since you broke up with your douchebag boyfriend."

Her eyes widen as if shocked that I noticed she hasn't been herself for the past few months. Tears spill from her eyes and streak down her face, and I want to kill that douchebag a hundred times over for hurting her.

The damn bouncer stands in the doorway, watching us.

"I don't want my dad to know. Please don't tell him." The puppy-dog eyes plead. "I quit, okay? You heard me quit, right? I won't go back, I promise."

I shake my head, steeling myself against the urge to give her anything and everything she asks for. Don Alberto would kill me for keeping something important like this from him. Hell, Don Alberto would kill me just for having seen his daughter practically nude.

Besides, Summer probably needs help. I have no judgement of strippers, but I know Summer well enough to suspect she's looking for attention from the customers at a strip club to fill some void. Allowing her to keep going down this path of self-destruction won't do her any favors. She needs someone to sort her out.

"I'm sorry, doll. You need guidance. If you ask me, someone needs to spank your ass to teach you a lesson in self-respect." Okay, I don't even know where that came from. It must be the Catholic school-girl outfit tweaking my inner dom.

Unbelievably, she gazes up at me with her big doe eyes and says, "Okay."

I cock a brow. *"Okay?"*

She swallows. "You can do it."

Why does she actually look hopeful about the prospect?

My cock surges against my pants, and my suit jacket suddenly feels too hot.

No. I can't be considering it.

I stare at her, trying to deny the appeal of bending her over and lifting that minuscule plaid skirt of hers to deliver a spanking. "You want *me* to punish you?"

She nods.

I push her back against the car, pinning her supple body between the BMW and my larger frame. She releases my shirt, and I grasp her wrists, pulling them together, tucked against my chest.

She stops breathing. Her nipples protrude through her blouse, and her lush lips part.

Christ. I want to take that mouth, possess her glossy lips. Own her. Show her what attention from a real man feels like.

I force some self-control. Her father is the don. The man I owe everything to. I can't degrade his daughter that way.

"No, *cara mia*. I can't."

Her face falls. "Why not?"

I picture her ass bared for me, my little princess to punish and protect. My gaze slides away, down the row of cars, and one corner of my mouth kicks up as I consider the truth.

"I'm afraid I would like it." I look back down at her, and she flushes, eyes dilating. Her chest rises and falls, drawing my gaze down to her apple-sized breasts.

"You would like punishing me?" Her voice cracks.

I look her square in the face, let her see the sadistic bastard I am. What she'd get if she unleashed my desire. "Yeah."

Damn, if she doesn't look excited. Fuck, if she doesn't push her abdomen back at my bulging cock, rocking her pelvis up. A low growl rises in my throat.

"I guess I'd prefer it that way."

Oh, this was too. Fucking. Tempting.

She blinks those big doe eyes. "Look, you know this would kill my dad. He thinks of me as his perfect little princess. His good girl. The one who's going to marry a lawyer or be a congressman's wife. Not only would it destroy him to know about this, but he'd be sick about the fact that you and... um..."

"Sonny." I supply the name of my soldier.

"Yeah, that you and Sonny saw me. That would really piss him off."

She's absolutely right about that. I put a finger under her chin. "Summer, I'm not kidding around about punishing you. It wouldn't be a game."

It's the only way I can justify it. That I'm actually trying to straighten her out, not perv on the don's daughter by enacting every kinky fantasy I've ever had about her.

She sucks on her lower lip. "Okay."

*Gesù Cristo.* I stroke her cheek with my thumb. I've never touched her this way before, even though I've always considered Summer to be mine—someday. As underboss to the LaTorre family business at the tender age of twenty-seven, I stand to inherit the kingdom—and that means I get the princess. At least in my mind. I'm pretty sure Don Alberto sees it differently, though.

"Please, Carlo?" Her voice sounds hoarse.

My breath stalls. When it starts again, my heart's taken off at a gallop. "You're giving yourself to me? For my correction?"

Does she have any idea what she's getting herself into?

She sucks on her lip again and nods. "Yes."

I look skyward. I should tell her no. This won't work. A) Don Alberto will kill me. B) Don Alberto will kill me again, and C) If I go home with her, I'll never want to leave.

But I'm already touching her. Her scent fills my nostrils, the warmth of her soft flesh ignites every cell in my body. I don't want to tell her no. I don't want to take her to Don Al and Carmen and tell them what I saw tonight, to bring hurt and disappointment to the couple who've become my new family. And now that I can practically taste Summer, I sure as hell don't want to give up this window of opportunity.

*Cogliere l'attimo.* Seize the moment.

I blow out my breath. Releasing her wrists, I step back and open her car door. When she turns to get in, I gave her delicious ass a smack.

I climb in the driver's side and adjust the seat back as far as it goes to make room for my long legs. "You're going to get me killed."

She unbuckles her high heels and toes them off. "Guess I'll have to make it worth it."

# Chapter Two

*ummer*

Carlo doesn't speak on the ride to the apartment he and my father helped me move into. I steal glances at him as he drives, noting the firm set of his square jaw, the furrow between his brows. Is he actually mad at me? Or just acting stern on behalf of my father?

I was surprised to hear his opinion that I need help. I thought I've been putting on a decent front since I broke up with John. I didn't know Carlo paid any attention to my mental state. Knowing he does sends a shot of longing through me so deep and drastic that part of me wants to tell him to pull the car over, so I can run away. Because he's right—I *am* fragile right now. And it wouldn't take any coaxing at all for me to fall hopelessly for the guy I've been secretly lusting after for the past four years.

He pulls up in front of my apartment and parallel parks in a tight space without having to maneuver the car back and forth. But Carlo pretty much does everything well. At least from what I've seen. He probably wouldn't treat me with scorn because I'm horrid at parallel parking, either. Carlo is never derisive like John. No, I'll bet he's secure enough in his manhood that he wouldn't need to pick apart his girlfriend to make sure she measures up. Or to cheat.

I open the door and climb out in my bare feet. My injured foot throbs from wearing the high heels.

I tug my short skirt down. Funny how what felt empowering and sexy in the club now seems shameful. At least it does until I catch the appreciative once over from Carlo when he meets me on the sidewalk.

Ok. He's not going to shame me. He likes what he sees.

Which means... this punishment might be more pleasure than pain.

Then again, it might not. I suspect one of the reasons Carlo has risen to power so quickly in my father's organization is his ruthlessness. I've even heard it mentioned he has a sadistic streak.

So pleasure for him. Pain for me.

I can work with that. I'm a dancer—we're natural masochists.

Carlo escorts me up the stairs with a hand at my lower back. I like the way it feels—gentlemanly and courteous like we're a couple. Like he's not leading me upstairs to do terribly kinky things with me.

The door to my place is thick and solid. My dad had it replaced for security measures, complete with a heavy-duty lock. Carlo still has my set of keys and doesn't bother to ask which one opens the door, just picks one and tries it. He chooses correctly. The door swings open, and he gestures for me to enter first.

I set my purse and heels down. Carlo slides off his tailored Italian suit jacket and drapes it over the back of a chair. When he slowly rolls up his sleeves, the butterflies dancing in my stomach take flight.

This is really happening. He plans to punish me. And enjoy it.

I wonder why that idea turns me on.

He walks over to me, a glint in his eye that I don't recognize. Dark and serious. Dangerous. He reaches for the top button on my blouse and unfastens it.

Oh God. The flesh between my legs clenches and lifts.

"Wh-what are you doing?"

"I'm going to punish you in the state of undress you were in at the club." His voice is dark and velvety. He stands so close, I can see the stubble of his five o'clock shadow in contrast to the soft pillows of his sensual lips.

I gulp air to clear my head. Hot. This is super hot.

Carlo's deft fingers move down my buttons then pull my blouse down over my shoulders. I shake my arms out from it.

He twirls his finger in the air, indicating I should turn around.

My heart thuds against my chest. I turn then look over my shoulder at my father's soldier. The young man who came in and instantly made a place for himself. Carlo's the relation of a relation, sent to America when things got too hot in Sicily if I understand correctly. Not that anyone has ever said as much to me, but that's what I've gleaned from overheard conversations.

Carlo's expression remains unfathomable, but I see heat in his eyes as he reaches for the zipper at the back of my skirt. God, he's handsome—olive skin, green eyes, dark, wavy hair worn on the longer side for a man. He stands six foot two and is built of solid muscle but moves with feline grace.

Heat swirls in my pelvis, flushes up my torso and chest. The skirt falls to my feet in a puddle. I stand in nothing but my white lace G-string and bikini top, goosebumps rising on my flesh.

Carlo takes my elbow and guides me to the arm of my overstuffed sofa. "Bend over."

My panties grow damp. I look at the rounded cushion. While I understand what he wants from me, my body won't move. I stand frozen, watching as he slowly unbuckles his belt. Breath coming in short little gasps, I will myself to calm down. Hyperventilation wouldn't be a good look for me.

Carlo moves with his signature confidence, pulling the belt from its loops in one smooth motion. He turns it over in his large palm, examining the edges and weighing the heft and thickness. I have to wonder how often he's done this. How many other women? He definitely seems like he knows what he's doing.

When his attention returns to me, he frowns. He winds the buckle end of the belt around his fist. "When I give you an order," he says, his voice low and dangerous, "I expect it to be obeyed."

My nipples tighten at his threatening growl, but for a moment, I'm suddenly not sure about any of this. I don't know this Carlo–he's acting so different from the charming, easy-going guy who sits at my parents' dining room table on Sundays. I'm not sure whether I want to go through with it. Whether I trust Carlo. How serious he is about this.

He steps closer, right into my space and wraps his hand around my nape, pulling my face right up to his. "Don't be scared, Summer," he says softly, his beautiful hazel gaze locked on mine. His clean, masculine scent filled my nostrils. "I know what I'm doing."

That part I believe. He definitely seems to relish this role. The guy's a kinky bastard, for sure.

"I'm going to take care of you."

My hands come up to his chest, the chiseled muscle of his pectorals standing out in stark relief. I stare at his sensuous lips, the sturdy, clean-shaven jaw, the scars that only make him more appealing—a thin line under his left eye, the slight crook in his aquiline nose, the scar on his left ear. I'm not sure how using his belt on my ass is *taking care* of me, but somehow, I believe him.

"You know you can trust me, don't you, *principessa*?"

I melt against his sturdy frame. Again, it seems like Carlo actually cares about me, and the need in me that produces burns like a knife through my gut. I have to harden my heart against his intoxicating interest. Just because he cares doesn't mean...well, it could mean anything. Carlo's a player, as far as I can tell. He's never had a girlfriend. I'm not sure he ever has more than one-night stands when it comes to women.

So maybe that's what this is. I'm cool with that. Anything to make him keep the secret about my job at The Candy Shop.

He releases me and tilts his head toward the arm of the sofa.

Stomach fluttering, I fold my body over it, presenting my ass to him. Having him fully dressed while I lie bared to him heightens everything.

He picks up my wrists and bends them behind my back, gently pinning them there.

"Carlo?" My nerves resonate in the syllable.

"Was this what you wanted, *principessa*?"

I relax a little more. He's verifying my consent. There's nothing to be afraid of. Just a little pain at the hands of a very hot man who will enjoy delivering it.

I learned pain is pleasure the first time I put on pointe shoes. I can definitely take it. More than that, I will probably love it.

"Yes," I affirm, my uncertainty gone.

He swings the belt, and the leather slaps against my flesh. I gulp and squeeze my cheeks together. Three seconds later a line of pure fire registers.

*Carlo*

If all my blood hadn't rushed south to my dick the

first moment Summer suggested I punish her, I would know I'm crossing a line that can't be uncrossed.

I have the don's daughter stripped down to a bra and panties, folded over the arm of her sofa, and I just laid a gorgeous red stripe across her perfect ass.

But even if I wanted to—even if I were capable of pulling back—it's too late now. I am all in with Summer LaTorre.

She wants me to give her a spanking? Hell, yes. I'm the man to do it. I've been on a tight leash with this girl for the past four years, and the tether to my control just fully snapped.

"This is for disrespecting yourself and your family." I slap the belt across her ass again. The G-string makes a pretty sight threaded between her cheeks, as do the twin welts I laid down. Looking at her makes my cock ache.

I've spanked my share of women—I definitely like to play bossman in the bedroom—but none like Summer. She's special—a class act. Smart, sassy, drop-dead gorgeous. She used to be confident before that *coglione* of an ex-boyfriend did a mind-fuck on her.

I bring the leather strap down across her buttocks again. I go easy on her—allowing her flesh time to warm up before I increase the speed and intensity.

Next time I spank Summer, it will be an intimate, over-the-knee spanking with my hand on her bare ass. No, wait. There won't be a next time. At least, there shouldn't be. Summer isn't mine.

Except every part of me rebels at that idea.

Isn't she? Clearly, she's offering herself up to me right now.

I continue slapping the leather down with a regular rhythm, giving her time to catch her breath between each one. When her ass turns a rosy shade of pink, I increase the intensity.

Summer lets out little cries and tries to roll away, but I hold her by her wrists.

"Hold still for your spanking, Summer." I use my velvety dom voice. "You asked me to give this to you."

She pants a moment. "Sorry."

My dick surges against my pants.

Damn. I suspected that under her sass, she'd be sugar-sweet. She was always standoffish with me, which was fine because the boss' daughter is one hundred percent off-limits. Courting her would've had me evicted from Don Alberto's organization faster than an eject button. Part of me wonders if she understood that—knew better than to flirt with one of her father's men, for their own good. I like to think so, anyway. Because over the years, I've caught her looking at me in a way that said she's as attracted to me as I am to her.

"You have ten more. I want you sore enough to remember this lesson tomorrow."

She shoots a nervous look over her shoulder, and I give her hands a squeeze to reassure her. The room fills with the sound of leather slapping flesh and Summer's little cries. I watch her carefully to make sure I don't go too far. By the time I've given her three strokes, she starts saying, "ow" and "I'm sorry" and "Carlo" in the cutest pleading voice I've ever heard. I'm ready to come just from spanking her.

I drop the belt and rub her heated flesh.

God, it feels so delicious. I shouldn't be touching her so intimately. Shouldn't be seeing her almost naked ass like this, but I wouldn't trade this experience for anything.

I pull her up, sweeping an arm under her knees to scoop her into my arms. Her breath catches, and then she tucks her face into my neck, which I love almost as much as I loved punishing her. I carry her into her bedroom and lay her down, sitting beside her.

She turns her face to me. I say nothing, just burrow my fingers into her thick, glossy hair, stroking it and massaging her scalp.

"You okay, *principessa?*"

She nods. "Yes. Thank you."

I don't know if she's actually thanking me for the punishment, but the idea of her liking it, of asking for more, makes the sadist in me roar to the surface.

"Did you enjoy it?" she asks.

The corners of my lips kick up. "Yes."

I try to get my head back on my shoulders, though. "This wasn't for me to get my kicks, though, *cara mia*. I...I care about you. I hate to see you making choices I think you're going to regret."

Tears spring into her eyes, and her lips tremble. I gather her back up into my arms and run my thumb over her lower lip. "You and I both know that you aren't right. You've lost weight, you're jumpy, and if you're spending your free time stripping, I doubt your studies are going well."

The tears spill down her cheeks. "Carlo—" she chokes.

I wait, but she doesn't go on. Resting her cheek against my shoulder, she finishes crying, letting me thumb away the tears as they fall.

She looks fucking beautiful, even with her eyes red and puffy. I don't mean to do it—taking advantage of her in this state would be cruel, and then there's the issue of her being the don's daughter. But her lips look so damn kissable. Without my permission, my head lowers, and I claim her mouth.

It's not a soft kiss, either. I go in hot, with the tension of four years' frustrated desire burning behind me. I slide my tongue between her lips as I hold her head in place for my plunder. At the same time, I catch her breast, crushing it possessively, sliding my hand inside her little bikini top and thumbing her nipple.

I almost jizz when she opens to me, lifting her face and kissing me back. Her tongue darts out, and I lose whatever control remains. I abandon her breast and go straight for her core, fingering her over her panties and, when I find them damp, slipping inside.

I stroke her dripping pussy, running two fingers along the length of her slit twice then pushing my middle finger inside her.

She jerks and arches, breaking the kiss, but it isn't shock written on her face. It's lust. And damn if her knees don't fall open in a clear invitation for more.

I mold my hand to her mons, using the heel of my palm against her clit as I stroke inside her. I add a second finger. Then a third.

Summer arches and rocks her pelvis into me, pushing for release. Her hands clutch around my neck, her head drops back. The tingling burn of her fingernails pressing into my flesh makes my cock throb. I wrap my fist in her hair and tug her head back while I pump my fingers in and out of her dripping pussy.

She thrashes underneath me, her legs sliding up and down as wanton noises escape her lips.

I finger-fuck her harder, letting my knuckles bump into her with force until her vocalizations reach a high-pitched keen. She cries out and, clutching at my fingers between her legs, shoves them deeper and holds them in. Her muscles spasm around my digits, squeezing and milking them, making me wish it were my cock inside her.

Five seconds, ten. Her orgasm goes on and on. When she finishes, she looks up at me with glassy eyes, her expression dazed. I ease my fingers out and kiss her again, showing no mercy. I'm not through with her. Not by a long shot. My brain conjures all kinds of images involving her stripped naked and bound, at my mercy. But...no. I need to get control. This can't happen.

Summer isn't mine. She's about as far from mine as a girl can get, considering she's the boss' daughter. And I just disrespected her in a multitude of ways. And the fact that she let me...hell, that bothers me more than anything else. Because if she's selling her body for dances down at

The Candy Store, chances are good she's looking for some kind of outward validation from men. So her giving herself to me isn't about an attraction between us—it's about her post break-up neediness. I shouldn't have taken advantage. Summer is still on the rebound—she definitely doesn't need me to add to her confusion.

Besides, I want Summer for keeps. And I probably just spoiled any chance I have to make that a reality.

* * *

*Summer*

My body buzzes from the unexpected orgasm, my mouth and pussy tingling, swollen from being so thoroughly taken. My heart patters against my chest with a strangely lightened beat, as if one encounter with Carlo added an optimism that's been missing since my breakup with John.

I blink up at my gorgeous...what? He's like family, but we actually aren't related at all. And *friend* doesn't seem to be the right term after what just happened. But he's not my lover or my boyfriend either. And he certainly is beautiful. His moss green eyes and dark, curling lashes make him movie-star sexy.

God, I remember all those nights after he first moved in with us. I was just seventeen—still in high school. He came in like a long-lost son. Played shadow to my dad. Quickly became his right-hand man.

Everyone watched, concerned my Uncle Joey would feel usurped, but it seemed to me like Joey was relieved. I don't know the inner workings of the Family because they don't discuss things with the women in the family, but we still know how things work. Where people stand. The hierarchical order of the made men.

Carlo came when my father needed someone he could trust and lean on. Someone to mold.

My mother loves him, too. He's charming and respectful. He praises her cooking and helps her with any little thing around the house—like carrying in her groceries or emptying the trash.

I'm the only one in the family who doesn't fawn all over him, and the only reason I feign total disinterest is that I'm afraid if I spend any time with him, I'll end up throwing myself at him. And that would put him in an awkward position with my dad.

Kinda like what just went down.

A furrow develops between Carlo's brows as he gazes down at me. "We'll add this to the list of things we're not telling your father, no?"

I have to laugh. Yeah, my dad would probably kill Carlo if he found out about this. "Agreed."

My blood still heats with the memory of his fingers pressing inside me, and the way he ordered me over the arm of the sofa. Carlo oozes masculinity, authority, and power, with that ever-present hint of danger. Well, they say a girl falls for a man like her father. Carlo certainly has many of the same qualities. And he comes in such a beautiful package.

He looks at me, his expression serious. "Summer, tell me something."

*When can we return to making out? How about now?*
"What?"

"Have you—? Do you do this often?"

I stiffen, glaring. What in the hell is he asking me? Is he judging who and how much sex I have? I draw my hand back and slap him.

Carlo catches my wrist before my palm reaches his cheek. He moved lightning-fast, reminding me he's a fighter, a dangerous man. His tight grip immediately loosens, and he brings my hand to his lips for a kiss. "Next time you raise a hand to me, you'll find yourself standing in the corner with a plug in your ass." His lips quirk and lids droop like the idea turns him on.

My eyes fly wide, and my pussy clenches. Jesus, Carlo truly has a kink. How did I not know this about him? Then again, why would I? People don't just talk about their sexual proclivities at the Sunday dinner table.

His words jolt me into equal parts lust and annoyance. My palm still itches to slap him, which he must know, since my wrist remains caged in his strong fingers.

"Are you trying to slut shame me?"

He releases my wrist and sits back. "No. I—" He looks uncomfortable. "I'm sorry, *bambina,* it was a stupid thing to ask."

I frown, not willing to let it go. "What did you mean by that?"

His forehead creases with regret. "I guess I'm the bastard who's hoping no one else has taken advantage of you the way I just did."

I flush. Did he take advantage? I didn't view it that

way. He didn't get off—I did. The way I see it, he administered the punishment we agreed upon and then gave me a little pleasure to go with it. It didn't seem like such a bad bargain to me. So what's his problem? Is he fishing to find out if I'm seeing anyone?

"I haven't been with anyone since John."

His shoulders relax. Reaching to cradle my face, he touches his forehead to mine. "No hard feelings?"

I'm not sure if he means about insinuating I'm a slut, taking advantage, or the punishment itself, but it doesn't matter. Even if I were steaming mad, it would be impossible to stay angry, centimeters away from Carlo's glittering hazel gaze.

"No hard feelings." Hurt feelings, maybe, but I'll get over it.

He pulls the covers out from underneath us, then pats the bed. I crawl under them. *Buona notte, bambi.* Dropping a kiss on my forehead, he tucks my bedspread up to my waist. "I'll drop your car back in the morning, okay? Do you have anywhere you need to be?"

I shake my head, pushing away the sharp disappointment at his departure.

He cups my chin and lifts my face. "Are you okay?"

A flush travels up my neck. Does he mean is my ass okay? Because, well, it still stings. Or does he mean is my pride intact? Not really. But yeah...the orgasm went a long way to help.

"Look at me, *bambina.*"

*Damn, that Italian accent always melts me.* If possible, I flush even more. With great effort, I lift my gaze.

His dark-lashed eyes hold warmth. He strokes my cheek with his thumb. "Are you?"

It doesn't matter, suddenly, that he bent me over the sofa and spanked me like a naughty schoolgirl. Or even that he believes he took advantage of me, which really means he has no interest in pursuing a relationship. Because the way he's looking at me shows he cares, and that makes up for everything else.

I turn my cheek into his hand and close my eyes. "Yeah. I'm okay."

I get another forehead kiss–which I relish–and he leaves.

Holy hell. I can't believe what just happened. How much I enjoyed it. That I want more.

Of course, this may be a one and done thing for Carlo. If I hadn't already known he was a player, his kinky expertise tonight proved it. I shouldn't hope for a repeat.

Shouldn't want to keep the spotlight of his attention aimed on me.

But now that I've had a taste, I'm addicted.

I need more from Carlo.

More dominance.

More attention.

More everything.

Too bad he's forbidden to touch me. Too bad my dad would kill him if he found out what we did tonight.

And worst of all–too bad I'm willing to risk that if it means I get more of Carlo.

# Chapter Three

Carlo

The cold metal of a gun muzzle presses against my temple.

"You fucked her, didn't you?"

I blink up at my brother in the dim room, cold sweat trickling down my ribs. "Who?"

"My girl. Summer. You fucked her."

I move to sit up, but Mario pushes the gun against my head with bruising force, pinning me in place. "I didn't," I croak. "I didn't mean to..." I reach out to touch the gun, and then I'm grabbing it away, pointing it at a terrified Ferdi, whose face I already bloodied.

"I was just following orders, kid." Ferdi has the gall to call me kid. Well, he had the gall to attempt to kill his own cousin, too.

"Whose orders?"

"Mario's."

. . .

I shoot up out of bed, the gun I keep beside the bed already in my hand. I peer into the darkness, my shirt drenched in sweat.

*Gesù Cristo.*

Four years, and the dreams still haunt me. Not that I had any doubt about what inspired this one.

I betrayed Don Alberto by fooling around with Summer. No matter how I try to frame it that I was doing her a favor, I debased her. Scrubbing a hand over my face, I walk to the shower and turn the water on cold. I'll be taking cold showers from now on until I get the image of Summer LaTorre's face during orgasm out of my head. Which may be never.

I towel off and dress in a pair of jeans and black t-shirt. Picking up my phone, I call Sonny. "I need you to meet me at Summer's."

"No problem, boss."

"I'll text you the address when I'm ready, and then I'll expect you there in twenty minutes. Got it?"

"Sure thing."

"Listen, Sonny. You tell anyone who we saw last night?"

"Absolutely not, boss."

"Keep it that way. You hear? Not a word to anyone, not even in the Family, *capisce?*"

"Loud and clear."

"Thanks, Sonny. I'll see you in a bit." I hang up and text Summer. *On my way.*

She doesn't reply. Well, if she's still asleep, I can always wake her when I get there. I head out of my brownstone and get into Summer's BMW. The car smells like her—a rich, vanilla scent, exotic and feminine. Unbidden, images of Summer bent over the arm of the couch flood my brain. The memory of the way she squirmed, moaning in my arms as I plunged my fingers in and out of her makes my cock harden, so I have to adjust myself in my seat.

*Stop thinking about her.*

But that seems to be an impossibility. The harder I try, the more she infiltrates my every pore until I breathe her in with each inhalation. I grind my molars and park the car, glancing up toward her window. At the front door, I push the button for her apartment.

"Carlo?"

"Yeah, it's me."

The door buzzes, and I swing it open. I remember Don Al having a fit over the fact that she didn't have a live door person for security here, but Summer insisted on this place because her best friend Maggie lives in the same complex. In the end, Summer won out, mostly because Don Al liked her being close to her friend. What he didn't like was knowing her boyfriend at the time would be spending the night.

Thinking about her douchebag ex makes my fists clench. I offered to teach the guy a lesson when Don Al had told me what happened, but Al refused. "Believe me, I'm thinking the same thing, but no. Carmen would kill me for interfering that way. She wants our kid to be normal—not part of the Family business. It was one of her stipulations when we married. So I'm gonna let it lie.

Unless he shows up in her life again. Then I'll kill the *coglione* myself."

"I can hassle him a little—you know, let the air out of his tires or key his paint job."

Don Al grinned. "I'm supposed to be letting her grow up and solve her own problems. But if his car got towed or something, it wouldn't be any sweat off my back."

So I had the *stronzo's* car towed. Not that it taught Douchebag any lessons, since I didn't get to claim responsibility. Still, I liked giving the *coglione* a headache.

Summer opens her door wearing a minuscule pink cami and boy shorts.

My cock hardens at the sight of her breasts shifting beneath the thin fabric.

She catches me looking, and her nipples pop out, as if eager for my touch. My fingers itch to touch them, squeezing and pinching them until she writhes for more. I wonder if she's the sort of girl who could come from breast play alone.

Stop. *Now.* I shake my head to clear it.

"Come on in." Her gaze dances across my face like she's nervous. "I made you some coffee."

So she *did* know I was coming. She made me coffee but didn't put any clothes on. Which meant she wanted me to see her that way. My hard-on worsens. I purposely avoid glancing at the sofa where I bent her over last night.

She didn't just make coffee, she brewed a *caffe latte* with her own fancy espresso machine. Something warm fills my chest. Does she remember that I hate American coffee? Or is this just the way she likes it?

She offers the cup. Once more, she fails to meet my eye.

I close my hand around hers, trapping it around the warm mug. "Summer."

She swallows and lifts her gaze.

"You don't have to be embarrassed. Not with me." I pull her closer, keeping her hand prisoner as I take a sip of the frothy milk-topped liquid.

Her lips part. Glossy lips. She put on makeup for me. The urge to throw her over my shoulder and carry her off to her bedroom comes on fast and hard. I'd rip her clothes off and spread her legs...

I shove my dirty thoughts away.

"You promise you're not going to tell my dad?"

"Cross my heart, *bambina*. You promise you're not going back?"

She nods.

"You're going to get yourself back on track?"

Her gaze slides away, and my heart squeezes for her. Where in the hell has all her confidence gone? I want to kill her ex all over again. Maybe have a few words with her parents, too, for shoving the business degree thing down her throat after her injury sidelined her dance career. I want to take her back to my place and help her sort out her shit. But none of those things are going to happen.

She pulls her fingers out from under mine. "Look...I'm not even going to try to explain to you why I started stripping because you're not going to understand."

Her words lance me through the chest. "Try me."

She shakes her head, a stubborn set coming to her shoulders. "I'm not going to do it again, so don't worry. You did your job."

Fuck. Did I inadvertently hurt her? Made her think I was only doing it for Al?

Setting down my coffee mug, I cage her against the counter, resting one hand on either side of her. "*Piccolina*, I work for your father, yes. We're like family, you and I. But..." I swallow, unsure what exactly I mean to tell her. That I've always had a place-holder in my heart for her?

Her breasts shift, begging to be licked, teased, tortured. Punished.

"I know I should stay away from you..." my voice sounds hoarse. *Did I say that out loud?*

She draws in a sharp breath.

I brush the backs of my knuckles along her arm, exploring the smoothness of her skin. "Would you believe me if I told you—" I stop. This time, I can't meet her eyes. I swallow and look to the side.

Somehow caution returns. Reason returns. Now is not the time to seduce Summer LaTorre. She's on the rebound. I want to win her fair and square.

I force myself to take my hands off her and step back. "I'd better go." I hold her keys up and set them on the table, not even trusting myself to hand them to her. "Call me if you need me, okay?"

Yeah, I'm running like a nancy right now. Scared of a beautiful, off-limits girl and my overwhelming desire to take her in every manner of speaking.

* * *

*Summer*

I lean against my kitchen counter, my heart pounding. What just happened? What was Carlo going to tell me? He wanted me? Or he couldn't be with me?

I scoot off and drop to my left foot, favoring the right. My foot stiffened during the night, making it hard to walk without a limp.

After I finished physical therapy, I returned to dance classes at Tisch School of the Arts. I could make it through the beginning barre, but once they move to "across the floor" exercises, I had to stop because the pain became too much. I had to take an incomplete in all the movement classes, which meant my dance major wasn't going to happen. At my mom's insistence, I changed my major to business. Now, I don't even have time to get myself back in shape and rehab my foot. I figure returning to dance is impossible, but that doesn't mean I don't still want to be a dancer. Without dance...*hell.* I walk to the bathroom and turn on the shower.

Without dance, I don't even know who I am.

I suppose it isn't John's fault I ended up stripping at The Candy Shop although I still refuse to see it as something negative the way Carlo does. I might have been filling a bigger void, though—the need to be on stage, to have my skills admired. Stripping a far cry from making serious art, but the sexual electricity made up for that part. I was still moving to music, still improvising, creating. The energy I received from the men gave the same thrill I got from performing for an audience.

I peel off my jammies and twist to peer at my ass in the mirror. I still have a few red lines. Reaching back, I run my hands over my butt. I've lost a little muscle since my injury, but I could still hold my own in an ass competition. I always thought of it as my best *asset*. Heh.

I pinch some of the red areas, but the soreness has disappeared. Just a few twinges on the surface.

My core still clenches every time I think about last night. I want more of that side of Carlo. But was that it? Was the key drop-off the end of our steamy encounter, never to be mentioned again? Because I don't think I can forget it so easily. In fact, I suspect I'll be thinking of nothing but Carlo for a long time in the future.

My phone buzzes with an incoming text. It's a group chat from some of the women in my study group. Business students, not dancers. They're going out clubbing tonight.

I'd said I couldn't go because I thought I'd be working at The Candy Shop, but I guess I'm available. It doesn't sound all that fun, but that's just because I don't know them that well. I sort of lost my friend group with the breakup with John. Well, that's not true, I'm sure they all still consider themselves friends with me, but I don't like going out with them anymore because he might be there.

I guess the Candy Shop was filling a social void as well. Maggie lives with her boyfriend, Pete, so they don't go out much. When they do, it's with the same group of friends that John belonged to, which means the atmosphere would be beyond awkward if I went along.

I sigh. I won't create a new social life staying home and moping. I text back, *My plans fell through. I'll meet you guys there.*

# Chapter Four

*C*arlo

I double-check the security cameras trained on the table and outside the door. Two soldiers wait outside the warehouse to keep an eye on the parking lot. Five more play security inside.

Sonny and Vince are my main guys. Sonny's a solid soldier. Vince is a dick. A cousin of Al's who definitely resents the position I've created for myself here. I always watch my back with him. Hell, I watch my back with everyone. My own brother tried to kill me back home. I know all too well that no one is safe in this business.

No one will be cheating at high-stakes cards on my watch or knocking off the participants. Running the weekly high-roller game is one of my more pleasurable duties. I enjoy the exchange of big money, the tension brought by high stakes. I like the character study my customers offer.

I have regulars. Ordinary guys with extraordinary

gambling problems. Lawyers, investment bankers, real estate agents. I have criminals who come in a rare meeting of the underworld. A guy from the Russian *mafiya*, a Cuban gangster, a mean-looking white guy who's somehow involved with the Russian. Sometimes a few of our own drop in.

The special knock set up for today's game sounds— two long, three short. I open the door to peer out. The Russian mobster, Alexei Kaloshov, stands there, looking lethal and high on uppers of some kind.

I step back to allow him entry. Alexei isn't the hand-shaking sort. He's more the type who would pull a knife and stab you if you accidentally jostled him. He wears a designer button-down shirt, open two buttons at the collar to reveal a tattoo of a dagger going through his neck.

From what I understand, the Russian *mafiya* are decorated with prison tattoos, and every one of them have a symbolic meaning. The dagger through the throat means the wearer committed murder, or would kill for hire, and the drips of blood are for each victim. Alexei's drips extend beyond where they are visible, but I suspect there are a lot. Too many, even for a mobster. The guy has a murderous vibe, and he uses drugs, so I always keep a close eye on him.

Sonny stands behind the table, ready to take his money and give him chips.

I let in several more guests, all clients I expect or at least know. Nine men show up and take seats around the large wooden table in the warehouse chosen for this week's game. In a matter of five hours, we transformed one section of the industrial space. A fine Persian rug lies on the floor, and the solid carved oak table sits in the middle. A stained-glass chandelier dangles mid-air over the table, suspended from the rafters by two twenty-foot chains. The chairs are cushioned red leather. Drinks are provided in crystal glasses with ice, served by a cocktail waitress in a hot outfit. Small speakers are strategically set around the room, and they play Sinatra on low volume.

The knock sounds again. I open the door and blink. Gio, one of the younger soldiers, stands there with a white guy. Make that—*stands there with a cop*. I have nothing to go on other than the guy's short hair and steady gaze, but my instincts say it loud and clear.

I don't open the door any wider. "What's up?" I ask, ignoring the stranger and focusing on Gio. The only question in my mind now is whether Gio knows he brought a cop.

"Hey Carlo, how's it going?"

I don't answer, just stare the guy down.

Gio shifts. "I brought a friend." He jerks a thumb at the cop. "Is there a game?"

"Nope. No game tonight. Maybe next week." My eyes slide to the cop, whose gaze remains steady.

Gio looks confused. "Oh, I guess I had it wrong?"

"Yeah. You had it wrong."

Gio rubs his face as he turns and scans the parking lot, taking in all the signs that the game is, indeed, happening. He isn't the brightest guy on the street, but fortunately he isn't completely stupid. "Okay, cool. I guess I'll see you later."

"Yeah. I need to see you tomorrow, actually. Meet me at Angelo's at ten." The Italian deli serves as one of our meeting places for business.

A trace of fear shows in Gio's face, but that doesn't necessarily mean he's guilty. He just understands something went wrong. "Sure thing, Carlo. See you in the morning."

I ignore the other guy until he turns around, then I watch him until they both get into Gio's car and drive off.

After the game, I'll get the feed from the camera and run the guy's photo. I need to know what I'm dealing with.

* * *

Summer

I weave through the crowd of drunken college students at the nightclub in the city. There's a large group of business students here—at least a dozen. Coming out sounded good at the time, but it feels hollow now.

I got dolled up, dressing skimpy for attention. I suppose I have an exhibitionist streak. Or maybe it just makes up for all the times John lifted a critical eyebrow and told me what was unflattering about my outfit or which body part looked fat.

I might've seen the light and left him sooner if I hadn't also had my dance career destroyed by the broken foot. I jumped down from the stage into the orchestra pit after a student performance one night. The pit was lower than I expected and the impact broke five bones in my foot. Now I have a little metal plate holding together the pivotal cuboid bone, and even after months of physical therapy, I haven't recovered the flexibility or strength.

I have to face the fact that I will never perform professionally—my dream since I was eight years old. My mom pushed the business degree, saying when I recover, I'll have the know-how to run my own dance company or studio, but I don't even know if that will be possible.

Plus, I hate business classes. Truly hate them. I have zero interest in business management. But it probably doesn't matter because at the rate I'm going this semester, I'll fail out, anyway. Which would kill my mom.

I wonder what my dad would think. He said very little about the whole thing. Sometimes I speculate whether he'd back me up if I set against my mother. But they've always been such a unified front—it's hard to say. And yeah, I'm a little old to let my parents run my life, but when they're paying for everything, they sort of retain that right.

"Come on, Summer, we're getting shots." One of my new friends tugs me toward the bar.

I follow, taking my turn with one shot of tequila then another. It slides down my belly like fire and hits me fast, reminding me that I haven't had much to eat today. The gaggle of business students head back to the dance floor, and I join them.

A good-looking guy sidles up, giving me an appreciative sweep of his eyes. He works his way into the circle my friends made, and they allow him. After a couple dances, he offers to buy me another drink.

I definitely don't need one, but what the hell? He's buying. I trail him to the bar and order a Cosmo. Only then do I get the creepo vibe.

* * *

*Carlo*

Sonny and Vince count the take for the night—twenty large. Not bad for a night's work. I pay them both their shares and lay out stacks of bills for the soldiers who worked security.

My phone vibrates, and I tilt the screen to see who's calling. Frowning, I swipe the screen. "Hey doll." I purposely don't call her by name, so the guys won't pay attention. Why is Summer calling at one a.m.?

"Hey Carlo, I need a favor." Her words sound slightly slurred.

Fear spikes in my chest. Cops showing up and Russians with happy trigger fingers never ruffle me, but thinking about Summer in danger turns me cold.

"Pay the guys out," I say to Vince, pushing the piles of cash in his direction and standing up. To the phone, I say, "Anything, babe. Where are you?"

"I'm at a club. I–I don't think I can drive, and this creepy guy is stalking me. I'm in the bathroom."

I grab my jacket and slide it on. In a low voice, I say to Sonny, "I need you to get the feed from the front door over to Joey to ID the guy with Gio."

"You bet, boss."

"Which club?" I ask Summer, stepping out the door.

"Five-oh-four."

"I'll be right there. You just stay put, do you hear me?" I stride to my Mercedes SUV and get in, slamming the door.

"Okay."

"I'm serious, do not leave the bathroom." I jam the key in the ignition and start the car.

She lets out a drunken giggle. "Yes, sir."

*Gesù Cristo.* If I weren't so nerved up about her well-being, those two words would make me rock hard. Summer La Torre playing submissive to *me.* Is that why she called me? I shake my head to push away the thoughts crowding my brain.

"Summer, I'm going to hang up now. Do not come out of there until I call you back. When I do, I'll be standing right outside the door, *capisce?"*

*"Yep, got it."*

I end the call and screech through the streets to reach Summer, ready to kill the asshole who has her hiding in the bathroom.

An agonizing thirty minutes later, I arrive, hand my keys to the valet parking attendant and pay a ridiculous cover charge to get into a club that will be closing in thirty minutes.

I push my way toward the back, looking for the bathrooms, eyeing every male who comes between me and that door. No one appears to be loitering around.

Too impatient to call her, I tap on the door and push

it open. My heart stops when I see Summer—my girl—sitting slumped against a wall, her head leaning back, her eyes closed.

"Hey," a girl shrieks.

Summer's eyes flutter open, and her face breaks into the delayed grin of inebriation.

"Get out of here," the offended customer squeals. "I'm getting a bouncer."

"Summer." It comes out like an exhale. I take two steps into the room and hold out my hand to haul her to her feet. She's wearing a body-hugging dress so short it barely covers her ass and shows every curve. She looks gorgeous, but I want to kill every man who saw her in it tonight. And she definitely isn't wearing a bra or panties underneath. I scowl. "Let's go."

A bouncer heads toward us as we emerge, but I narrow my eyes, giving him a deadly look. The guy stops his advance. Smart man.

"Where is the guy?" I demand. I'm going to shove his balls down his throat for messing with my girl.

Summer twists around, scanning the club with an unfocused sweep. "I don't know."

It doesn't matter—I'm being stupid. I'm not going to knock out a guy's teeth in front of her, no matter how much I might want to. That lacks class. Getting Summer out of here is priority number one.

"Never mind." I grit my teeth and lead her out of the club, where I hand my number to the valet guy.

Summer shivers as we wait for the car, the crisp autumn air far too cold for her outfit. I shuck my jacket, draping it around her shoulders. The valet driver pulls up and gets out. I beat him to open the passenger side car door and help Summer inside. Reaching across her, I buckle her seat belt.

"You're sweet." She rolls her head to the side and smiles at me.

"You might not think so when I'm through with you." I wink to soften the warning.

I don't mean it. I would never touch Summer without her consent. I would certainly never bully her. But she opened the door to my domination, so now I can't help the dom-talk from tumbling out of my mouth.

She makes a show of sitting up taller and folding her fingers in her lap. "Uh oh. I think I'm in trou-ble." She sings the last word, which is absolutely adorable. It also tells me she's into it.

I slam her door and walk around to my side.

When I climb in, she leans her beautiful face close to me. "Are you going to spank me again?"

"I'm not sure you'd even register it right now." I try to keep the amusement from my tone.

She sits back in her seat and folds her hands in her lap again. "Thanks for coming to get me." She sounds a little defeated, and now I wish I hadn't played hardball.

I expected more drunken sass. My chest tightens to hear the raw vulnerability in her voice. I reach out and brush my knuckles along her jaw. "I'm glad you called me, *bambina*."

She looks over, her eyes still not focusing. "Are you going to punish me?"

"We'll discuss it when we get home."

"Which home? Can we go to your place this time?"

I furrow my brows. "Why?"

"I don't like living alone." It comes as no more than a whisper, and it wrenches my heart. My baby doll is lonely.

I don't want to be the random guy she stuffs into her life to fill a hole, but I don't trust anyone else to be that guy, either. "Yeah, we can go to my place."

It's wrong. I'm going to get myself killed if I'm not careful. But how can I refuse her? I'm not made of stone.

We drive in silence, and she sobers by the time we arrive.

I unbuckle her belt and reach across her to push open her door. She climbs out. At first, I think she's stumbling on her heels because she's drunk, until I realize she's limping.

"Is your foot bothering you?"

She tosses me a rueful look and reaches down to take off her high-heeled sandals. "Yes."

"Why do you wear those things?" I swing her up into my arms where she seems to fit. She smells like cranberries and liquor and her own tantalizing scent, sweet and intoxicating.

She lets out a surprised breathy laugh and tucks her head into my shoulder as I carry her up the stairs and into my apartment. Her weight bothers me—she's too light in my arms. She's never been anything but slender, but she can't weigh much more than a hundred pounds now.

I reach the living room and deposit her on her feet.

She looks around my apartment with a curious glint in her eye. Sitting on my leather sofa, I pat my lap.

She comes over, a flirtatious smirk around her lips. "Am I sitting or lying down?"

The corners of my mouth kick up, and I pull her over my lap. "Definitely lying down."

This is how I wanted her the first time—stretched out over my legs, her punishment intimate. I slide her minuscule dress up and discover I was right—she isn't wearing anything underneath. "Where in the fuck are your panties?" I growl. Was she trolling at the club and just caught a bad one? The thought makes me grit my teeth. I want to go back and gouge the eyes out of every man who even looked at her.

I bring my hand down on one of her cheeks with a loud slap.

"I didn't like the way the lines showed."

"That's because this dress is too damn tight." I know I'm being a dick. A woman should be able to wear whatever the hell she wants. But I can't think rationally when it comes to Summer.

"The answer is not to go without panties, it's to pick a new outfit."

I know, total *stronzo*.

I slap the other side, then repeat the action. "Or, if you have to wear that dress, bring a bodyguard. *Me*."

Apparently, the alcohol hasn't numbed her ass because she wriggles, gasping and jerking. I find a rhythm, loving the feel of her gorgeous ass under my hand.

"Carlo!" she squeals.

I stop and rub her ass. "Summer, you called me to pick you up. You must have wanted this punishment. Am I right?"

She doesn't answer.

I continue rubbing away the sting. "You didn't call Maggie or your dad to come and get you. You didn't call an Uber or a cab. You called me. I think you want me to take you in hand."

She rolls her hips on my lap, making my dick even harder.

"Listen, *piccolina*. If you tell me no, I won't touch you, and I won't say another word about it. But I think you want this. Am I right?"

For a moment, I think she's going to say no, which means I've read this whole situation wrong. Which means I've degraded the don's daughter.

I'm definitely a dead man.

But then she makes my year. "Yes."

Triumph floods my veins. "Good girl."

# Chapter Five

*Summer*

S I'm not sure I agree with Carlo that I want a punishment, but I definitely want whatever he's offering.

So he must be right. I called him because I want him to be my knight in shining armor. And yeah, some part of me must have hoped he would punish me. I squirm and wriggle over his lap, struggling to absorb his steady slaps without a fuss and becoming aware of his growing erection prodding my hip.

My own lady parts have been slippery wet since the moment he pulled up my dress and bared my ass. Actually, since the car ride, when he made it clear he'd be spanking me again. Carlo's dominance makes him all the more attractive in my eyes. What did he say he would do if I slapped him again? Put a plug in my ass and stand me in the corner?

Um, wow.

I masturbated to that dirty thought this morning.

Heat builds on the surface of my ass as he continues to spank me. I'm not even sure what the spanking is for. "Bad decisions," he says.

"Surrender, Summer."

One word. It sends a shiver up my spine, flips my belly like a pancake and makes my pussy leak moisture.

I want to obey him. But how does one surrender to a spanking? I bury my face in the sofa and bite the cushion, willing my butt cheeks to unclench.

"Good girl."

His words made my insides slithery and warm.

I force myself to remain still. And find it impossible. Every time his palm connects with my ass, every muscle in my body tightens up. Still, I try to minimize my squirms.

"That's it, Summer. Surrender."

His words make me dizzy. My clit throbs. One brush, and I reach orgasm.

I spread my thighs a little, inviting him to touch me there.

It turns out to be a winning strategy.

"That's it." Carlos stops spanking and kneads my ass and thighs, his touch commanding and possessive.

I lift my ass. *Please touch my lady bits. Please.*

He grips my ass cheek then swipes his fingers between my legs.

Yep. Just one brush. My thighs clamp closed and ripples of release rock through me.

His fingers fist in my hair, and he pulls my head up. "Did I say you could come, *principessa*?"

Another wave of orgasm makes me buck. I choke on a gasp.

"Did I?"

My eyes can't seem to focus. "N-no."

He lowers my head, massaging away the sting of my scalp. "No, I didn't." His silky voice enters my body, rich and warm. "Next time you'll ask permission first. *Capisce, bambi*?"

*God, that accent.* The caress and heat of his fingers makes me purr. My pussy contracts again. "Yes, sir."

He caresses my heated ass. "I like it when you call me *sir*."

I lift it up. Despite my orgasm, I still ache for more, my pussy slick and swollen, clit needy for more of his touch.

"Summer." He sounds choked. He slaps my ass. It's a lighter slap, not so punitive as before, but still stingy on my already raw flesh.

I arch my ass back. "More."

"Oh God," he groans.

He starts spanking me again, a quick flurry of spanks that make me grind against him, desperate for everything he has to give. The stinging reverberates when he stops and drags a digit down the crack of my ass. His thumb meets my back pucker at the same moment two fingers plunge inside me.

My body jack-knifes up, back bowed, head lifted to emit a guttural cry.

"Do I need to punish you back here, babygirl?" He massages my little rosette with circles as his fingers continue to plunge in and out of my pussy.

My brain scrambles, and I become incapable of answering his question. I both want it and don't want it at the same time. Abruptly, the room swoops as Carlo helps me to my feet, cradling the backs of my thighs in his large hands. He squeezes them possessively. His eyes are heavy-lidded and dark, hungry.

I can't even comprehend how we arrived at this territory, this burning heat between us, this new game. Two punishments, I suppose. If I knew all it took was a couple screw-ups to induce Carlo into showering his dominant masculine attention on me, I would have misbehaved long ago.

He wraps his arm around my waist and draws me even closer between his knees. One thumb comes to my trimmed pussy, and he lightly strokes my outer lips, which glisten with dew.

My legs tremble, threatening to buckle. How can he do this to me while I stand? My head swims.

His thumb finds my clit, and I buck at the contact, electricity shooting down my inner thighs. Carlo holds me firmly in place, torturing me with a slow circling rhythm that leaves me panting.

"Carlo—" Moisture dribbles onto my thighs.

"Spread your legs."

I whimper.

He removes all contact with me, leaving me bereft.

I ease my feet apart.

"Hands on your head."

My clit throbs, my nipples ache, desperate for his touch. I interlace my fingers and place them on the top of my head.

He nudges me to step back and stands. "If you move from this position, I will take off my belt and spank you until you scream. *Capisce*?" He speaks the last word as a low, suggestive rumble in my ear, having moved around me.

I shiver.

He slaps my ass. "Answer me."

"Yes, sir. I mean, no, sir, I won't move."

He squeezes the offended cheek. "Good girl."

I glow at the praise.

I listen to the sound of his footsteps retreating, straining to hear his movements, but not daring to turn my head and watch. He's way too far away. I need him closer, need those hot hands on my body again.

He returns and brushes a hand over my ass, trailing it down my thigh. "You're being a very good girl, Summer," he rumbles.

Foolish pride makes my head swim.

He circles me and resumes his position on the couch. In his hand, he holds a bottle of olive oil. Patting his knees, he flicks his eyebrows.

Heat spikes in my core, floods down my legs to curl my toes. I fold myself back over his lap, offering my ass back up to him. I hear the scrape of metal as the bottle's lid comes off and the trickle of oil slides down my crack.

"Carlo?" Panic begins to set in.

"Shh, *bambina*. I won't hurt you." He returns to massaging my anus, working the oil into the ring of muscles, then applying slight pressure. "When you've been naughty, doll, your ass gets punished on the inside and out."

O. M. G.

"Um..." My whimper sounds wanton.

"Open for me." His voice deepens with the command.

But my body doesn't know how to open for him. Everything tightens to resist the intrusion.

"Exhale, Summer, and take me."

I blow out my breath, and my sphincter relaxes, allowing—*oh God*—his thumb to enter.

I moan, the degradation of being taken in this way, as a further punishment, equally hot and embarrassing. I love it. The humiliation makes my pussy weep and my body open to him.

He strokes two fingers along my slit, bringing me to the edge of another orgasm with just one swipe.

"Please, Carlo..." Every muscle trembles now, every cell seems to be on the verge of combustion.

He pushes his thumb deep into my ass, then shoves two fingers in my pussy as he withdraws his thumb. Rocking back and forth, he plunges in and out of each hole in opposition. The sensations overwhelm me, make me delirious with need. I rub my face on his sofa cushions, my toes curling and uncurling as the inevitable explosion nears.

"Ask me for it."

"Please, Carlo, please..." What does he want me to do? Oh yes... "Please let me come, please may I—"

"Come for me, Summer." He buries his fingers in both holes and stays there as I contract around them, coming harder than I've ever come in my life.

And I suspect I've only brushed the surface of the places Carlo might take me.

\* \* \*

*Carlo*

Through my lust-induced haze, it occurs to me that I've done it again. I didn't mean to defile Summer, but here she lies, bare-assed over my lap with my digits buried deep in both holes.

*Classy, Carlo. Real classy. Way to court your future wife.*

I ease my fingers out, trying to force my raging hard-on to deflate. Summer probably notices it pressing into her hip.

I squeeze the back of her muscular thigh, finding it hard to regret anything I've done with her. Because there's no mistaking her response—Summer's a submissive. She may even be a masochist, but either way, her body responds to my natural dominance. It would have been all right if she weren't kinky. For a woman like Summer, I would have suppressed my nature and given her tender love-making, but discovering this side of her makes her all the more desirable.

Which doesn't help my problem with the don.

Somehow, I'll have to figure things out because I want Summer for keeps. I'd hoped to someday be given Summer. To have earned her. But this will negate any chance of that.

So what now? It doesn't happen often that I find myself unsure of what move to make next.

Tugging her dress down, I pull her up into my arms.

Summer's flushed face and glassy eyes give her a just-fucked look, which makes me want to toss her on her back and complete the ravishment.

She rubs her lips together and looks at me with heavy lids. "Are we going to talk now? I'm not even sure what that spanking was for."

Definitely submissive. I lean my forehead against hers. "No? Why do you think I spanked you?"

Her forehead crinkles. "It's not my fault I attracted a stalker." There's no heat behind her words, more confusion.

"Were you at that club alone?"

"No, I went with friends."

"Well, where the hell were your friends while you were hiding in the bathroom?"

She gives a half-shrug. "I guess they left me at some point."

I want to fire all her friends and get her some worth keeping. "They didn't say goodbye?"

She nibbles her lip. "They might have...I was a little drunk for a while there."

A good reason for her friends not to leave her there alone. *Cristo*.

"You were at a nightclub looking hot as fuck in that dress—*with no panties*—alone, and a little drunk. I seriously want to punch a wall right now."

Her jaw juts forward. "Don't you dare tell me I asked for it by wearing this. Because that's victim blaming, and—"

"No, *bambina*. But I'm surprised you didn't have twenty stalkers waiting outside that bathroom door for you. But it's not your fault they're assholes. Your friends aren't worth a damn, either. Listen...here's the rule, and I expect you to remember it—don't wear that dress out again without me at your back. Or better yet, wear it *only for me* in private."

The retort she appeared to be gathering falls away when my words register. Her pretty lips part. "For you...?"

A prickle of heat makes me unbutton the collar on my designer shirt. Am I going to stake my claim on her now? Or keep things loose and undefined? Her wide copper-colored eyes contain something resembling hope. My heart picks up speed.

*Cogliere l'attimo.*

"Yeah." I slam her with a possessive stare. "You heard me."

She meets my challenging gaze and swallows.

"I think you need looking after."

"And... you're the man to do it?"

The corners of my lips kick up. "That's right."

"So...what? You're like, my bodyguard?"

I shake my head. "I'm your keeper." I stand up from

the couch, keeping her cradled in my arms. Carrying her to the bathroom, I plunk her down on the counter and wash my hands.

She sits docile and sweet, but a charge of anticipation runs between us.

I have a toothbrush still in its package under the sink. I pull it out of the wrapping and squeeze a line of toothpaste on it. Handing it to her, I say, "brush."

"Bossy." She feigns a pout but takes the toothbrush.

I make quick work of my own teeth and hand Summer a washcloth for her face. She scrubs, obediently. When she finishes, I cover her hands bracketing her sides on the countertop with my own, pinning her there. "Listen to me, *bambina*. I'm going to take you to my bed now, if you agree. But know this--if you spend the night here tonight, when tomorrow comes, I'm not letting you go. You're going to stay here with me and live under my rules, so I can take care of you."

It's bold. Bordering on lunacy. If Don LaTorre finds out, I'm a dead man. But having Summer here in my apartment makes me reckless. Unwilling to let her go.

Her breath stops.

I've gone way too far, but hell, I can't see any other way around it. I'm not going to stand around and watch Summer free-fall anymore. And if I claim her, I'm not going to do it half-assed. I'll make her mine. Worship that body of hers. Figure out what's going on in that beautiful head that's making her act out this way.

"Is that all?"

Her answer surprises me. No reaction to my

proposal? "No, that's not all. I back up all my rules with discipline." The corners of my lips tick up. My dick presses against my zipper. "So you'd be giving yourself over to me. Mine to punish. Mine to pleasure."

Summer's eyes dilate. She lowers her gaze to the bulge in my pants. "Do I get to pleasure you, too?"

I almost jizz in my pants.

Did she really just accept all my terms and then offer to blow me?

Gripping her hair, I tip her head back and lean in close, skimming her jaw with my lips. "You won't have a choice, doll."

Of course, it isn't true, but I can't resist the test. How will my little submissive respond? Does she trust me?

She shivers, and her eyes roll back in her head. Licking her lips, she says in a whiskey voice, "When do I start?"

*Summer*

Carlo steps back, his lids lowering. "Take off your dress."

My pussy clenches, and suddenly the orgasm he gave me wasn't enough. Catching hold of the edges of my skin-tight dress, I shimmy it off, over my head, and toss it on the floor.

Carlo makes a tsking noise. "Not like that, *amore*." He points at the dress. "Pick it up."

I slide off the counter and bend to pick it up.

"With your teeth."

I freeze. My face heats even as fresh desire blossom in every cell of my body.

Wow. Carlo really is into humiliation. Apparently, I am, too, because the flush of heat pouring through my body makes me feverish. Dropping to my hands and knees, I lower my head and pick up the dress with my teeth.

Carlo bends and slaps my upturned ass. "That's fucking hot, *bambi*. I like you at my feet. Way too much." His smile is feral. Shadows fall on the planes of his face, accentuating the angles, so he looks like he's been carved of marble. A Roman God.

Every third second, I experience misgivings at letting myself be debased this way, but then I circle back to one fact: this is *Carlo*. Sexy, debonaire, mysterious, and one hundred percent trustworthy, at least in my experience. I've already allowed him to discipline me, and he hasn't left me hanging in the wind. He proposed I move in with him. Never mind the fact that we've never even had a date.

Carlo unbuckles his belt, a sight that leaves me breathless. Doubling it, he swings it, catching my buttocks without any force. It stings, but doesn't cause real pain. "Crawl for me, angel. Into the bedroom." He swings the belt again.

It strikes like a kiss—the slap of leather somehow becoming a caress.

I take off, crawling on my hands and knees, my dress still between my teeth.

Carlo follows, whipping me.

My pussy drenches my inner thighs, swollen and tingling. My breasts sway, heavy, nipples aching.

I find the bedroom. A king bed stands in the center, draped in a charcoal print bedspread. All the decor is simple yet expensive.

"Stop. Kneel up." Carlo positions himself in front of me and unbuttons his pants. The bulge in his elegant suit trousers hasn't decreased since my punishment.

I lick my lips, dizzy with desire for him. I reach out, then stop, hand in the air, wondering if this game is like Simon Says, where I have to wait for him to tell me what to do.

"You may touch it."

I lunge for the zipper on his trousers, tearing it open. Pulling his pants down enough to free his length, I grip the base of his shaft and flick my tongue over the head.

The growling noise that comes from Carlo's throat makes me air-pump my hips.

A drop of pre-cum issues from his slit. I lick it off then swirl my tongue under the rim. His cock swells even bigger, straining toward my mouth. I look up and meet his hooded stare. When he caresses my cheek, I lean into his steady hand.

Holding his eyes, I part my lips and take him all the way into my mouth, tracing his veins with my tongue.

"Summer." His voice is rough as gravel. "I never thought—"

I pop off to give him my full attention.

He gives an impatient shake of his head and fists his

hand in my hair, pulling my head to his cock again. "Never mind. Don't stop."

I take him into the pocket of my cheek, taking care with my teeth. I drag my fist up and down the length of his cock in concert with my mouth, milking him.

Carlo growls again and pulls out. "Get on the bed, naughty girl."

I scramble up, tripping when my stiff foot impedes my eager launch.

Carlo catches my arm and steadies me, pulling me against his chest for a savage kiss. His tongue punishes, sweeping into my mouth, tangling with mine. He sucks my lower lip into his mouth, nipping it before letting go.

As I come up for air, the room spins.

Carlo slaps my ass. "On the bed."

"Yes, sir," I giggle.

In a flash, he rolls both our bodies, so I lie on my back, and he straddles me. He pins my wrists up by my head. And then he stops. Indecision plays on his face.

"Carlo—" I bring my fingers to the buttons on his shirt, working swiftly to undo them.

He stares down at me, his eyes dark with heat. "Listen to me, *cara*."

I draw a breath at the bossy way he speaks to me, my nipples tightening into hard buds. His hardened cock presses against my belly, but when I lift my hips, he ignores my efforts.

"Are you sure about this?"

"I-I think so."

He shakes his head. "No *think so*. You're either all in,

or I find some restraint before we take this too far. I meant it when I said I wouldn't let you go. If you stay in my bed tonight, you belong to me."

I suspect my dad may take issue with this arrangement, but I can't muster any complaint. I want to be owned by Carlo.

"*Capisce?*"

"*Capito.*" My nonna is Italian, so I understand the language but don't speak it fluently. Still, many words and phrases have infiltrated my speech.

He looks surprised, as if not expecting me to agree. "Yeah?"

I thrust my hips again. "Yes, sir."

His cock jerks against me.

"I will take good care of you," he promises.

He looks so sincere that my belly does a full somersault. Or maybe my entire body does because I get lightheaded. Once again, this is so close to my fantasies, it hurts.

Carlo's a player. A full-blooded Italian man who's left a wake of satisfied women behind him. I can't take any promises from him seriously. Not to mention the fact that I doubt my parents would approve. But using him to regain my confidence while on the rebound isn't criminal. If what already transpires between us is any indication, sex with him will be out of this world. So I'll have my rebound fling and heal my wounds. No harm done. As long as I keep my heart locked up tight.

He lowers his head and kisses me again. This time, his lips are soft. Not quite so demanding. Almost tender.

My heart squeezes as if he tied a string around the middle and pulled too tight.

"So those are my conditions, *principessa*. Do you accept?"

I wriggle under him, still trying to tempt him into more. "I already said I did."

"I want to be sure you understand. I'll be keeping my thumb on you. You won't be going back to that job."

I roll my eyes. "I already agreed to that, Carlo."

"You won't leave this apartment without my permission except to go to classes."

My body heats at the idea of being his prisoner. "How do I earn my freedom?"

His feral grin turns wicked. "You'll have to be a very, very good girl."

My nipples and clit throb in time together. This is dangerous. More dangerous than my hare-brained idea to take off my clothes at a strip club. But the temptation outweighs the risk. I need this. My body needs this. I've gone too long feeling ugly and completely unappealing.

"I'll be good," I whisper.

He pulls off the shirt I unbuttoned and shucks the white t-shirt underneath it. His chest ripples with beautiful muscles, making me weak with desire. "Roll over and give me that ass." He backs off the bed and removes his pants.

More flutters in my belly. What does he mean by that? Is he going to spank me again? Or take me anally? Jesus, I've never done that before. Despite my qualms, I roll over.

I hear the sounds of him removing his pants, and then the mattress dips as he rejoins me on the bed. My ass and back twitch as I wait for his next move.

The crinkle of foil reaches my ears as Carlo opens a condom. "Put your wrists above your head."

I obey, and he pinions them in one large hand. Lying on my tummy with my hands captured, I am completely at his mercy. There'd be no way to control our lovemaking, save lifting my ass for him, which I do.

"God, Summer. You're fucking beautiful." He brushes my long hair to one side and lays kisses along my bare shoulder. The flick of his tongue teases me, his warm breath sends shivers of excitement through me.

Heat flushes every part of my body, and that's before the head of his cock nudges at my entrance. My pussy's entrance, thank God. He doesn't want my ass.

My juices are so slick that he slides right in. I groan at the sensation of being filled by him, the bump of the head of his cock on my inner wall. My body opens to him, more wet and ready than I've ever been.

He lowers over me, separates my wrists, and interlaces his fingers over mine. The intimate gesture turboboosts my heart rate. His breath comes hot on my neck and he bites down. The sensation shoots me over the edge. My pussy clamps down on his cock and my back arches. I squeeze his fingers tight as my inner walls contract with wave after wave of pleasure.

"Responsive little thing, aren't you?" Carlo sounds amused. He hasn't come yet, I realize with a stab of guilt. The score is Me: two orgasms; Carlo: zero. He pulls out and rolls me onto my back. His large palm flattens between my breasts and drags down to my tummy.

I suck my belly in, not liking anyone to touch me there.

He stops and frowns. "Are you really pulling in your belly?"

I stare back at him.

"Do you think it's too big?"

Flushing and hating the direction of the conversation, I look away.

He grips my waist with both hands and drops his head, laying four light kisses across the taut skin. "You have a warped perception of your body, sweetheart. You're too skinny as it is. I'm going to have to turn Italian grandmother on you and fatten you up."

I roll my eyes, but his words send warmth into my chest.

He kisses the hollow of my throat, and licks down to my nipple, which he takes between his teeth. He nips it then laves away the pain with his tongue. "Open those perfect thighs for me."

My legs part of their own accord. It seems I am incapable of refusing Carlo anything.

He sinks into me, rocking his pelvis with slow, deep thrusts. "Play with your nipples."

My doubt must show on my face because he says, "You heard me, *bambina*. Pinch them."

My pussy contracts around his length. I bring my hands to cup my own breasts. It feels dirty and self-indulgent, but the fact that Carlo not only gave me permission, but commanded it, makes it okay. I squeeze my nipples between my thumbs and the sides of my index fingers.

"Harder."

My eyebrows shoot up.

He plows into me with so much force my head slides close to the headboard. He braces my shoulders and slams in hard again. "I said, *harder.*"

I catch my breath, holding back the orgasm that screams just around the corner, ignited by his dominance, his harsh command. I pinch my nipples and squeeze hard, pulling them out and gasping.

"God, you're sweet." His voice sounds rough.

I pinch my nipples again.

Carlo somehow senses I'm about to come because he growls, *"Not. Yet."*

My eyes widen, and I stare up at him, slightly chastised, waiting for his next command.

He thrusts into me, speaking on each instroke, "You will...wait...until...I...give you...permission...to come. Got it?"

I clutch the sheets, my fingers twisting in them like claws. Holding off my orgasm seems like an impossibility, but he holds me, trapped in his burning gaze as he pounds into me.

*"Now."* He thrusts into the hilt and stays there. Even through the condom, I swear I feel his hot cum spill.

A shudder goes through my entire body. My vaginal muscles spasm, inner thighs clench, lifting the arches of my feet. Carlo literally makes my toes curl. Every part of me continues to tremble as the aftershocks run through me. My head swims, eyes lose focus.

I collapse on the bed, thoroughly used, limp with release.

* * *

*Carlo*

*Gesu.* I never expected her to be so incredibly responsive. Hot and so damn sweet. A natural submissive. I must have known on some level because I've been attracted to her from the start, and dominating is my kink. But Summer's full of life, full of fire. She never gave me the time of day, other than breezy pleasantries. I would've thought she'd be hard to get, that winning her submission would be the job of a lifetime.

But here she lies, obedient and tame, in my bed. The cool, aloof little vixen I imagined would take elaborate courting already surrendered wholly to me without so much as a date.

I ease out of her and dispose of the condom. When I return, I pull the covers out from underneath her and flick them across her body, then settle beside her. She rolls into me, her hand on my chest.

I stroke her hair, run my knuckles along her cheek. So beautiful. So perfect. And so *not* mine.

Instead of minimizing the damage I've already done, I made a deal to keep her here, with me.

How do I think I can explain this to the don? *I hope*

*you don't mind, but I captured your daughter, and I'm keeping her prisoner to be my own personal sex slave.*

Yep. I'm fucked. Don LaTorre has been like a father to me. I respect the hell out of the boss, and would never do anything to jeopardize my position in the organization. Or so I thought.

But Summer just turned my world on end, and no matter how I try to shake out the situation, there's no way I can see out of this. I'm not going to send her away, not when she just gave herself to me.

I am still a *stronzo* for being the guy who's taking advantage of her when she's down. But at least I'm the only asshole. I won't let her get hurt. Hopefully, I'll be able to show her worth.

# Chapter Six

*Summer*

*I'm in high school, wearing my Catholic school uniform. John is there, flirting with my friends, teasing them by lifting up their skirts and slapping their asses. He turns to me with a frown. "Your skirt is too long. Why don't you wear it short, like theirs?" He jerks his thumb at my friends.*

*I unbutton the top button of my white blouse, trying to look sexier.*

*John folds his arms across his chest, looking at me critically. "One breast is larger than the other."*

*My hands fly to my breasts, and I cup them, squeezing my own nipples.*

*"What are you doing?" His face is screwed up with contempt.*

*I drop my hands, shame flooding me. "Nothing....nothing."*

. . .

I shake myself awake. Ugh. That sick sensation that has been in my belly for the past five months has returned in full force. Actually, that ickiness has probably been there for the past two years.

Well, fuck John. I never would've been good enough for him. His loss.

I look down at Carlo, and his glory of hard muscle and uncompromising lines, his masculine power no less potent in sleep. Just the sight of him makes me ache. Could a man like him be captured? I doubt it. The way he handled me last night and the week before tells me he has a thousand times more experience in bed than I do. And you only get that way with a lot of variety. Of course, John had a lot of variety and still never got me off. All this time, I thought I was defective. He made me feel that way.

*No one makes you feel.* That's what my best friend Maggie, with her studies in psychology, would say.

I slip out of bed, taking inventory of my body. Sore in all the right places. I slip on the dress from the night before and find one of Carlo's t-shirts in a drawer.

He rolls over at the sound and mumbles something in Italian. I catch the word *bambina*. He looks content. I sure as hell hope he's dreaming about me and not some other "baby" he has for a sleepover.

Pulling Carlo's t-shirt on over last night's dress and tying a knot at my waist so I didn't look obscene, I slip on my strappy heels. Not the best walking shoes, but I could really use a latte.

I grab my purse, fishing out my phone. Maggie texted me. We usually have coffee together on Saturday mornings, so she might have already knocked on my apartment door and might be worried that I didn't answer. I hit the call button next to Maggie's name as I slip out the door.

"Hey, girl, how's it going?"

I step into the elevator and press the button for the ground floor. "You'll never believe it. Well, you might." I didn't tell Maggie about the first time with Carlo, but now—if his bedroom talk of last night can be believed—things are going to continue.

"What?"

"Well, I know you warned me something like this might happen." The elevator door opens, and I walk outside, heading down the sidewalk. The Starbucks locator on my phone shows one just a couple of blocks away. My foot doesn't love the walk, but sometimes caffeine requires sacrifice.

"Oh no, what?"

"No, no, it's not that bad. Last week Carlo showed up at The Candy Store when I was working. You remember, my dad's... um, employee?" I'm pretty sure Maggie understands what kind of biz my father's in, but the two of us have a tacit agreement not to talk about it.

"Oh, crap."

"Yeah. He pretty much hauled me out by my ear."

"Are you serious?"

"Mm, no, not literally. But pretty close."

"So what happened?"

My face heats. There's no way in hell I'm going to tell Maggie that Carlo took me home and, er, punished me. My ass clenches at the memory, accompanied by thrills of excitement. "So, um, he took me home."

Maggie must catch the awkwardness in my tone because she leaps on it. "Wait, wait, wait—are you telling me something happened?"

My naughty parts tingle with the memory of the way Carlo pleasured me. "Yeah."

"Wait a second." Maggie sounds mad. "He hauled you out of The Candy Store and then brought you home and had sex with you? What the hell? Because he assumed you were a slut just because you were dancing?"

I stop walking, annoyed. "No, he didn't bring me home to have sex. He brought me home—well, to...talk," I improvise. "And we didn't have sex. We just fooled around a little. After we talked." Yeah, you could call it a form of talking.

I start walking again as Maggie digests that.

"So, was it good?"

"Yeah. Really good. Amazing, actually. And then we, um, hooked up again last night. I spent the night at his place."

"O.M.G. Are you serious?"

I giggle. "Yep."

"And? Are you there now?"

"Yeah. Well, I'm walking to get coffee, but yeah. He said he wants me to stay with him for a while. I guess he thinks I need to get my shit together, and he wants to help."

"Well, I agree with him. But what's his motivation? Did your dad put him up to this?"

My throat tightens. I had the same thought originally, but Carlo swore he wasn't just doing it for my dad. "Uh, no. I don't think my dad would approve, actually. I'm not sure what his motivation is. I guess it's more sex. Which I'm totally up for."

"Summer—" Maggie's voice holds reproof.

"What? You're the one who told me I need to have a rebound fling. So this is my fling."

"Listen...this sounds too intense. Staying with him? That's not rebound sex. That's entering into a new relationship way too soon."

"It's not a relationship. Believe me, I know better than to imagine this is going to be anything permanent. But Maggie, the sex was good. Really good. I mean out of this world good. And he's not going to let me go back to stripping. So I need this."

"You're claiming more sex therapy?"

I grin. "Yeah."

"Girl, you're nuts." I hear the resignation in Maggie's voice. My plan has been accepted.

"Well, I'm not even sure it will happen. It might have just been the heat of the moment. I guess I'll see when I get back."

"Okay, well, keep me posted either way."

I promise I will and end the call. Entering the coffee shop, I order a macchiato for Carlo and a latte for myself.

*I'll take good care of you.*

The need those words produce in me give flight to kites of longing, tethered to my heart.

Did he mean it? Carlo's the type who would take very good care of a woman. Efficient and capable, he takes care of everyone in my family, from my parents to my nonna and all the other elders who adore him just because he came from the Old World.

But is he playing for keeps? Or just playing?

\* \* \*

*Carlo*

When I wake, Summer's gone. I heard her moving around but was so relaxed, still blissed out from the sex the night before I didn't want to wake. I didn't expect her to leave.

I pull on a pair of jeans and look around. Her purse isn't on the chair where it was the night before. I walk through the apartment. No Summer, no note. Where in the hell did she go? My keys are still on the counter, so she didn't take off in my car. She might have called her friend Maggie for a ride.

I look at my watch. Nine fifteen. And I made a date with Gio at ten. I can reschedule, but the Gio situation is important.

The door pushes open, and Summer slips in, holding two paper cups from Starbucks. Relief courses through me.

But we're playing a game here. She agreed to my

rules. To my punishment. And she's already broken a rule.

Lucky me.

I pull a stern expression. "What did I tell you last night about leaving this apartment?"

She makes a face. "I just ran down to Starbucks." She holds out a cup. "This is for you."

"Thank you." I accept the hot drink but set it on the table without tasting it. "What did I say would happen if you broke the rules?"

A lovely blush colors her cheeks. "Come on, Carlo. Don't be a hard-ass." Despite the protest, she takes a few steps closer to me. Damn, her obedience turns me on.

I crook a finger. "Come here, *principessa*."

"But I brought you a drink," she wheedles. Cute as fuck.

The corner of my lips kick up, and I reach for her face, stroking her cheek with my thumb. "I appreciate that doll, I really do. But when I make a rule, I expect it to be followed. You've earned another punishment."

Her eyes dilate, telling me her excitement matches my own.

"Unfortunately, I don't have time to administer it. So your punishment will have to wait until later."

Relief and disappointment war on her face.

I smile. "I'm going to take a quick shower. I can drop you at your place on the way to my meet-up, so you can get your things, and then we'll go pick up your car."

She looks adorable in my too-big t-shirt worn over her

tight dress. I can't help but reach for her, sliding the fabric up and down over the curve of her hips. She arches her breasts up and affects a flirtatious tone. "You're bossy."

I stroke along her thigh. "Get used to it, *principessa*."

She flushes and licks her lower lip.

In a half-second I'm all over her, yanking her soft form against my body and claiming that lush mouth. Her hands come to my shoulders, and she opens to me, kissing me back, leaning into me.

I break away and bite back a curse. "I'm going to be late if I don't stop touching you, *principessa*." I pick up her coffee and hand it to her. "Wait here. I'll be out in a minute."

Ten minutes later, I weave through traffic as Summer steals glances at me from under her long, dark lashes. A thread of tension emanates from her.

"Second thoughts?"

She tucks her hair behind her ear. "About what?"

"Being under my thumb?"

She flushes, a smile curving her lips. "I guess I was just wondering if that's what we're still doing."

I stop at a light and turn to give her my full attention. Or rather, to demand her full attention. "Yeah, that's what we're doing. I gotta figure out what to do about your dad, though, if I don't want to end up six feet under."

She worries her lower lip with her teeth. "I don't think we should say anything. About anything. Okay?"

The light changes, and I hit the gas. I should be relieved. This will keep me from getting my balls ripped off and shoved up my ass.

But I hate her suggestion.

Does it mean she doesn't think this thing will last? Well, why would she, anyway? Just because I proposed an insane scheme designed to keep her as my own doesn't mean she's wearing my ring.

*Yet.*

# Chapter Seven

Carlo

Gio sits at an outdoor table at Angelo's with two coffee mugs in front of him. He stands when I get out of the car, his eyes darting to the gun holster across my chest and up and down the street.

The idiot ought to know if I was going to whack him, I wouldn't do it in front of Angelo's, the outfit's hangout.

Gio licks his lips. "Hey, boss."

I give him a slight nod and slide into the seat across from him. "This for me?" I palm the ceramic mug.

He sits back down. "Yeah. Three shots of espresso. The way you like it."

I don't touch the drink. Poison isn't really the way of *La Famiglia*, but I wouldn't rule it out. "Appreciate it. So listen, Gio. Who was that guy you brought last night?"

Gio spreads his hands. "Listen, Carlo. I'm sorry. I thought it was okay to bring someone, but obviously, I shoulda checked with you first. I fucked up. I'm sorry." His words sound rehearsed.

"You didn't answer my question."

Confusion wrinkles his face. "The guy? He goes to my gym. We were talking one day, and he mentions how he likes to go to Vegas for high-roller games. I thought he'd be a good addition. I'm sorry."

I relax although I don't let Gio see it. His story sounds true. Still, I'm going to sweat him for being a *coglione*. "The guy looked like a cop to me."

"A cop?" Gio's look of confusion turns to one of alarm. He holds his palms out as if to ward away my anger. "Oh hey, I didn't know anything about that. He told me he works in real estate. Some kinda developer, I think. I thought he had money. Thought he'd be good for the game. But if he's a cop..." Gio's eyes take on a slightly crazed look, desperation mixing with ruthlessness. "I'll take care of him, Carlo. It's my mistake, I'll do it."

I give a sharp shake of my head. "You'll do nothing. First of all, we don't kill cops. Second, I'll handle it. *Capisce?* You'll do nothing."

"Are you sure? Because—"

"What did I say?"

Gio backs down immediately at my tone. "I got it, boss. I do nothing."

"And yeah, you don't bring a guest without checking with me first. In the future."

Gio exhales as if he wasn't sure he had a future. "I'm really sorry, Carlo."

I nod. "I know. We're cool."

Surprise flits across his face. "Yeah?"

"Yeah. But *cristo*, get your head out of your ass. Men at the gym are not your friends."

Gio bobs his head. "Right, right. I'm sorry. I fucked up. Big time."

I push to my feet.

"Thanks, Carlo. I appreciate your, uh, understanding."

I let that one go without acknowledgement, walking to my car and getting in. One question answered. Now to ID the cop and find out what he wants.

* * *

*Summer*

After I shower and dress, I call Maggie to come over and visit while I pack.

"We went to Toronto's last night." Maggie names the bar-lounge where our friends often go to listen to live bands and hang out. I haven't been there much since I broke up with John because it took a lot of getting psyched up in case he was there. The last time I went, I spent three hours picking out the perfect outfit and primping only to show up to a totally dead night with none of our friends there.

"Did John go?" I don't why I ask–more habit than anything. A pattern of thinking I haven't been able to break. Looping thoughts—I can't seem to stop. I have to say, though, that familiar locking in my chest when I bring him up isn't there this time. Something's changed.

I know exactly why.

It has everything to do with my beautiful Italian lover.

Maggie purses her lips. "Actually yes." I wait for her to say more, but she walks to the kitchen to help herself to a glass of water.

"And?" Jesus. Why am I still picking this scab?

"What do you want to hear, Summer?" She sounds exasperated.

"I know. I don't even care. I don't know why I'm asking."

"Are you sure you don't care? Here you are, getting packed for your sex therapy with a totally hot guy, who you claim you just had the world's best sex with, and you're asking about *John?*"

I feel slightly nauseous. She's right. I hate how wounded I was by him. It's not even about him—it's about my own feelings of self-worth. Somehow, they got tied up with him.

"I definitely don't care."

"I don't think you're over him. So maybe you'd better put the brakes on the new relationship before you screw things up."

The knot in my stomach twists tighter. Maggie's wrong. But even if she were right, I sure as hell am not going to give up this thing with Carlo. Still, I suspect she's hiding something, and that's why she doesn't like me asking. "Was he with someone?"

Maggie rolls her eyes and huffs but doesn't answer.

Ugh. I don't care. I *totally* don't care, except it twists the part of me that still feels inadequate. Not good enough.

"He *was*, wasn't he?"

"So?"

"Who was he with?"

Reluctance flits across Maggie's face. "Someone I'd never seen before. She looks like you, actually. Her name is Shelly."

I can't decide whether to be flattered or pissed that he picked someone who looks like me. Does it mean he really *did* like my looks, despite all the criticism? Or just that he has a type? Does he pick apart Shelly the way he pointed out all my flaws?

I experience a stab of jealousy—not for Shelly, but for my old life when I hung out at Toronto's with friends and had a boyfriend (even if he was a dick). Instead, last night, I was hiding from a stalker at a nightclub with no friends worth keeping.

Of course, the ending to the night had more than made up for it. I had Carlo's hot hands and lips and tongue all over my body. And I sure as hell wouldn't have wanted to be at Toronto's, watching John waltz in with a new girl on his arm.

I'm not jealous. This is just what it feels like to let go of the old me. My old life.

I turn to my closet and start pulling out clothes. "I don't even know how long to pack for," I complain, getting a little manic as I toss clothes from my closet into a suitcase. "I mean, is this, like, a week-long thing? Or just for the weekend? Or...?"

Secretly, I want it to be a forever thing, but that can't be what Carlo has in mind.

Like he said, my dad would kill him.

Besides, who would invite someone to move in permanently after having sex one time? Certainly not a player like Carlo. He hasn't lived with a girl in the four years he's been here.

Everything about this situation is just plain bizarre, including my own reaction to being punished by a hot and kinky alpha male. It's on the tip of my tongue to confess the kinky part to Maggie, but every time I start to say something, I bite it back.

Maggie's very liberal. And while she's sex-positive, she's also a feminist. I don't know if she would take Carlo's new self-appointed role as my keeper as kinky or old-world patriarchal. Plus, she might think my acceptance of all this is related to my damaged self-esteem. How can I explain the way my body turns to molten liquid every time he starts bossing me around?

How much I want to have him in charge of me.

Protecting me. Punishing me.

Pleasuring me.

"Just bring enough for the rest of the weekend. It would be weird to assume any longer, and besides, you can always come back and get more stuff Monday if you decide to stay, but Summer—" she levels me with a concerned-friend look—"this is all going too fast."

My gut clenches because Maggie's right. I'm being

impulsive and crazy. To assume anything long-term will come out of this thing with Carlo is laughable. "I'm just having fun. I promise." I cross my heart with my forefinger. "I deserve some hot sex right now."

A sympathetic smile stretches Maggie's lips. "You do."

"Do you?" Carlo's deep voice startles us both, and I shriek and whirl. His eyes glitter like dark jades, and while his expression is inscrutable, there's a dark, dangerous air to him.

Did he hear what I was saying? Well, it's not a lie. My face heats. "Don't I?" I reach for coy.

One corner of his lips lifts in a lopsided smirk. "That depends. Are you in the habit of keeping your door unlocked, so strange men can walk in at will?"

Excitement flaps in my belly at the scolding. He's looking for new reasons to punish me. To assert his will. It's a game he loves playing, and I love being his partner in it.

I dart a glance at Maggie to see how she takes the scolding, but she simply grins and looks between us as if fascinated by our exchange.

"You're not a strange man."

He leans in the doorway, his broad shoulders and tall frame as elegant in jeans and a t-shirt as it is in a fine Italian suit. "I could be."

"Well, I guess it's a good thing you're here to protect me, then."

"Hi Maggie." Carlo moves in to give her a cheek kiss, his European habit of greeting.

"Hi, Carlo." Maggie waggles her eyebrows in my direction when Carlo turns away.

I grin back.

"Well, I'll leave you to it, then. Call me later, Summer," Maggie calls as she heads for the door.

"See you."

Carlo stalks toward me, his eyes dark with intent.

I stand rooted to the spot, excitement sparking in every cell.

Carlo bends and tosses me over his shoulder.

I shriek and pound on his back, giggling. "What are you doing?"

"I believe I owe you a punishment, *principessa*."

I laugh and kick my feet in a show of resistance, but my giggles give me away.

As smoothly as if it were choreographed, Carlo drops me to my feet, sits on my sofa, and pulls me across his lap.

*Yummy.*

He peppers my ass with playful smacks. They're hard enough to sting, even through my jeans, but light enough to leave me needy for more. I lift my ass to him. He continues to warm it with quick spanks, then he lifts me to stand between his knees.

"Pull down your pants."

I flush, glancing toward the door. Maggie could walk back in at any second.

He jerks his head in that direction, guessing my thoughts. "Go lock it."

"Thanks." I exhale and dart over to turn the lock. When I return, my heartbeat kicks up speed.

Carlo reaches for the waistband of my jeans and tugs me forward, unbuttoning the jeans himself. Hooking his thumbs in the elastic of my panties, he pulls both down until they drop at my ankles, and I step out of them.

Feeling vulnerable, I practically dive over his lap, eager to hide my face in the cushions.

He runs his warm hand over my bare ass, caressing my curves.

I shiver.

"This is for leaving without permission this morning." He smacks my ass again, harder this time. Another slap. Then another.

I squeeze my cheeks together and wriggle.

"You might have thought I was kidding, but I wasn't. I'm completely serious. Until I'm sure you're back on track, I need to know where you are at every moment. You don't run to Starbucks, you don't go to the grocery, you don't take a walk without first asking my permission."

"That's...ridiculous," I pant, the pain starting to register now. Heat builds on the surface of my ass, tingling.

He stops and rubs. "You may think it's ridiculous, but it's a rule you're going to follow, or there'll be consequences."

I'm not sure I mind his consequences all that much. Well, I would if they were like that first punishment with his belt. Except even that experience was hot.

"Do you understand me?"

"Oof. Yeah, I understand."

He slaps the back of my thigh, which makes me yelp. "That is not the proper answer."

My brain muddles with dealing with the sensation, so it takes four more slaps before I yelp, "Yes, sir! Yes, sir, I understand!"

He stops and runs his palm over my heated cheeks. "Good girl. And now I want to have a talk about what you were doing at The Candy Store."

I start to push myself up, but he pushes me back over his knees and gives me a couple more slaps. "This is what I call an *over-the-knee discussion*. You're bared to me in a humbling position, so I can correct you immediately if I don't think you're being honest."

*Oh, God. Carlo is beyond kinky.* He's downright depraved. And I am freaking here for it.

He brushes a finger between my legs.

My pussy immediately plumps open, dripping wet for him.

"If you answer me well, I will reward you. If you fail to satisfy, your gorgeous ass is going to be rosy red. *Capisce?*"

"Yes, sir."

"Why do you want to strip?"

My clit pulses between my legs, needy for more of his touch. "It makes—I mean, made—me feel sexy." I have to admit, being over his knees where I don't have to look him in the eye and can hide my face makes it safer to share my feelings.

I expect him to scoff at my answer or at least discount the reason as unimportant, but he says nothing at all. He strokes my burning ass, tickling my inner thighs with his fingertips, but scrupulously avoiding my needy core.

"And I miss performing."

Again, no snort that stripping was a far cry from dancing professionally.

"It built my confidence."

When I don't add anything more, his fingers burrow into my hair, and he leans over, speaking into my ear. "Thank you, *cara*, for explaining it to me."

"Do I get a reward now?" I open my thighs as far as I can with the restriction of my jeans and panties at my thighs.

His finger brushes the outer lips of my sex again, making my inner thighs quiver. "Not yet, *principessa*." Another brush.

I gnash my teeth, my clit aching for his touch.

To my dismay, he pulls up my panties and jeans and helps me up to straddle his lap. Cupping both my breasts, he kneads one as he applies his teeth to my nipple through the layers of my thin t-shirt and bra.

I yelp.

"Do you feel sexy now?"

I flush and look down at the place our bodies conjoin.

He puts a finger under my chin and lifts it. "Do you?"

"Yes," I say softly. "You make me feel sexy."

He looks genuinely pleased. "Good." He squeezes my ass possessively. "My job will be to make sure you always know how incredible you are. How beautiful and talented. And absolutely perfect. Your job will be to obey. Do you think you can do that?"

* * *

*Carlo*

Summer wears a just-fucked look even though she hasn't gotten off yet. It makes me want to throw her onto the floor and ravish her in every way imaginable.

Her tongue darts out and licks her lower lip. "I don't know."

I smile at her honesty. "If you fail, I'll punish you. But I think you might enjoy your discipline as much as I like giving it, so that won't be so bad."

A gorgeous pink stains her cheeks.

"I won't let you fall, *principessa*. I'll always catch you. I may spank you until your perfect ass wears my handprint, but you'll be safe with me. Do you believe that?"

She drags her lower lip between her teeth. "Yes."

"If you need reassurance, if you need some sugar, even if it's in the middle of a punishment, you can always ask for it."

"What if I change my mind?"

"About what?"

She lifts one delicate shoulder. "About any of it."

"Are you asking me for a safe word?"

"Yeah, I guess."

I brush her jaw with my knuckles. "*Bambina*, I would know you were struggling long before you used a safe word. I'm going to pay attention to you. But if you want out at any point, just say that."

"Say what?"

"Say you want out. I would never violate your wishes."

Summer's shoulders relax. She lifts her eyes again, the coquette returning. I've seen more facets of Summer in the past few days than in the four years I've known her. Her submissive side is the most surprising, but I also love the sex pot, the ingenue, the vulnerable young woman. I love them as much as I love the sassy, stuck-up mafia princess who never gave me the time of day and expected my service when her father snapped his fingers.

"Carlo?"

"Yeah, baby?"

"Do you do this with all your...I mean—" Embarrassment scrawls across her face.

"I've played dominant before if that's what you're asking. It's my personality, and I like the fetish, too, but I could live without it if my girl wasn't into it." I meet her gaze, trying to convey that she's my girl. The one I would change everything to please, if she needed me to. That this isn't a requirement, even though I love it.

I stroke her cheek with my thumb. "But you are, aren't you, *tesoro mio*?"

The copper eyes lift. "Am I your girl?"

"You are. I thought I made that clear last night. You're mine now."

Her full lips quirk into a smile. "Yes. Yours to punish and to pleasure."

I return the grin. "That's right." I have a thousand wicked plans for both those activities. If Summer needs to feel sexy, I will make sure she does. I'll keep her turned on, objectified, worshipped, degraded and generally sexed every minute of the day until she learns how fucking desirable she really is.

That part seems easy. Figuring out how to handle the don is another story. Because I sure as hell can't run back to Sicily if things go south here.

# Chapter Eight

*ummer*
          Carlo carries my suitcases down to the street
          and drives me to his apartment. It's farther from
NYU, but I don't mind. I have a nice car. I valet park,
even in the city. My dad doesn't like me taking the
subway, so I'm well-practiced at driving in and out of the
city.

I'm thrilled to be staying with Carlo.

*You're mine now.*

The words pierce my armor like a flaming arrow.
They burn and cut. I want them to be true. God, how I
want them to be true. But how can they be? I sit next to
Carlo in the passenger seat of his beautiful car, which he
keeps neat as a pin, unlike my car, which is pretty on the
outside and a rumpled mess on the inside. Kinda like me.

What does Carlo mean by all this? Is he really trying
to "fix" me? Or just playing kinky games? Either way, I

shouldn't get too attached. He's not the kind of guy who plays for keeps.

Besides, it would be incredibly awkward if my parents found out. My mom would probably disapprove, as much as she loves Carlo. She wants a banker or lawyer for me. And my dad... he's a dangerous man. He's been a dick to every guy I've dated, but he would take personal offense to one of his own men touching me. He would see it as a sign of disrespect. A claiming what supposedly belongs to him. As if I'm a possession to be given or granted.

Which is why I plan on keeping the whole thing on the down low.

I study Carlo when he's not looking, admiring the proud angles of his bone structure. I wonder how he got the tattered ear. A knife? Bullet wound? Teeth? He's certainly a warrior. I wonder how many men he's killed.

He navigates traffic with ease, his hands relaxed on the wheel. I don't mistake the relaxed exterior for easy-going, though. His is a practiced calm; power and force rippling just below the surface. He's strong and capable, like my dad. I feel safe when he's near and sorry for anyone who gets in his way.

I understand all this about him by his presence, which is as familiar to me as family. And yet, what else do I know? For four years we've eaten Sunday dinners together, but I'm not acquainted with the real Carlo. And it seems he's been paying attention to me, which now puts me at a disadvantage.

"Why did you come to the States, Carlo?" Nothing like going for the heaviest question first.

Carlo's eyes slide sideways and move back to the road. He doesn't open his mouth to speak, and for a moment, I think he's not going to tell me.

"You want to know my secrets, *bambina*?"

Tingles flush across my chest, tightening my nipples, the idea of knowing his secrets exciting me. "Yes."

"Why?"

I rub the seam of my jeans. "Well, it seems like I don't really know you."

He arches a brow.

"Well, I don't. I know what you like to eat, or at least what you tell my mom you love. And I know you don't like American coffee, but other than that, what do I really know? I don't even know what you do for the organization."

Carlo frowns and opens his mouth, but I cut him off with a wave of my hand.

"I know we don't talk about that. But the problem is, what else do we talk about?"

Carlo's face has the cool, blank mask he always wears.

Why have I never before wondered what lies beneath it? "Cat or dog?" I quiz.

"What?"

"Which do you prefer?"

He smiles. "I have nothing against dogs. But I like cats, actually."

I laugh at his embarrassed look, as if it's some kind of

weakness to like cats. "I love cats. My mom's allergic, but I always planned to get a cat when I moved out."

"Why didn't you?"

"Maggie's allergic." Maggie was my first roommate—we were placed together in the NYU dorms freshman year. "And then John didn't like them."

It occurs to me that Carlo has a talent of offering very little and turning the conversation back to me. I press on. "How many girls have you spanked?"

He laughs. "I don't know—twenty? Twenty-five? Thirty? Contrary to popular belief, I don't notch the bedpost."

Even though it's as I expected, nothing stops the jealousy from clawing up my throat. Still, I press on.

"Have you had a serious girlfriend? I mean, you never brought anyone to my parents', but have there been partners?"

He gives a dismissive shake of his head.

"Why not?"

He shrugs. Another non-answer.

"Why did you come to New Jersey?" I try again.

He doesn't answer, and nothing changes on his face, but I sense the thread of tension my question draws.

"I won't tell anyone," I promise.

The corner of his lips lifts in that lopsided grin, but just as quickly as it appeared, it vanishes again. A furrow deepens between his brows. "My brother ordered me killed."

I would gasp, except I stop breathing altogether.

Now Carlo's knuckles tighten on the wheel, tension flexes his jaw.

"Why?" My voice cracks a little. I almost don't want to hear the answer.

Carlo pulls into the parking lot behind 504 and parks next to my car.

"I rose too fast in the organization. My father was dying. Mario thought I'd threaten his future as the Don."

My vision blurs, and I grip the dash as if I might fall out of my seat without it. "Carlo...I'm so sorry. That's awful."

He doesn't answer, but I suspect he has more to say.

I sit perfectly still, waiting.

"Sometimes, I think the same thing might happen all over again. If Joey wanted back in or if one of the older guys like Vince gets a hair across his ass. People don't like when a younger man holds more power. Your dad's healthy, though, so it hasn't come to a head."

He finally turns to look at me, and I must look shocked because regret washes over his face. He reaches out and strokes my cheek. "I shouldn't have told you any of that."

"No, I'm glad you did. I'm so glad." I unbuckle my seatbelt, wanting to get closer to him. Wanting to climb in his lap, despite the difficulty presented by the steering wheel.

He gives a surprised chuckle when I attempt it and allows me to nestle into him. "Why did you think I moved here?"

"I don't know—I thought you were hiding from the

law or something. But I realized it could be anything. I can't tell what goes on inside your head. I mean, I had no idea you were a sick bastard who likes to take his belt to —" I break off in a shriek of giggles as Carlo tickles me. "Safe word! Safe word." I press my elbows to my sides and twist to and fro. I'll take a spanking with his belt over tickle torture any day.

He keeps his fingertips pressing into my ribs but doesn't move them. Bending to bite my ear, he murmurs, "Frivolous use of the *safe word* is going to get you spanked."

I shiver, excitement darting up my spine. "Safe word."

HIs chuckle is rich and dark. He makes a tsking noise. "Bad girl. Get in your car. Drive back to my place and take your clothes off."

My pussy turns liquid at the authority in his voice. I never knew I had a switch that could be flipped so quickly. I've gone from zero to horned up in about two seconds flat. Never mind that it's the middle of the day, and I have a boatload of homework I ought to do.

"Yes, sir." I crawl off his lap and out of the car. Leaning my head back in, I say, "Safe word."

Carlo laughs again.

I shut the door and climb in the BMW my father bought me as a high school graduation present, tossing my purse onto the pile of stuff sitting in the passenger seat. Tomorrow I'll clean my car. If my jail-keeper gives me permission to leave his apartment, that is.

* * *

Detective Michael Bailey wakes to the low buzz of his phone alarm at five a.m. He flicks it off and rolls out of bed. His wife's side is already empty, which means she's up with the baby again. Slipping on a pair of running pants and a t-shirt, he pads out in search of them.

He finds them in the rocking chair in the living room, both his girls sleeping peacefully. Staring down at his daughter's tiny, angelic face and his wife's tender one, his chest constricts as love mixes with the sharp fear of losing them. Having a family changed everything for him. They are too sweet, too precious to lose. The contrast between their innocence and the horrors he sees on the street stuns him. Sometimes it seems like he lives dual lives—the hardened undercover cop working to bust open a sex slave ring and the man who has to put it all away when he comes home to them at night.

Jasmine sighs and makes a sucking motion in her sleep—air-nursing they like to call it. Her little cheeks have filled out since birth, and her thighs are starting to get chunky, too. Samantha calls her a "yummy baby" and pretends to eat her fat feet.

He resists the urge to drop kisses on both their heads, not wanting to wake Jasmine after Sam worked to put her back to sleep. He sticks his feet in his running shoes in the foyer and steps outside the house to sit on the stoop and tie the laces.

The air feels humid, but at least it's still cool at this hour. Standing up, he skips the warm-ups and goes straight to running, settling into a rhythm that brings focus to his thoughts.

His investigation of Alexei Kaloshov still hasn't yielded the location of the sex slaves nor who's next up the chain in the Russian mafiya. He heard a rumor they are coming from Chicago, but there is no proof of anything.

None of his attempts to make contact and attempt to purchase a slave have panned out. He still doesn't understand how he was made at the LaTorre's high-roller game, and that worries him. Is his identity known with them?

He runs until his thoughts have run out, and nothing but the sidewalk and the rhythm of his feet striking the concrete remain in his awareness. Until he circles back to his house and sees an elegantly-dressed man leaning against a Mercedes SUV outside his front door. His body goes cold.

He has no weapon—his gun is still locked safely inside. *Inside!* If anything has happened to Jasmine and Samantha...

Grinding his teeth, he approaches the figure, making out the face of mobster Carlo Romano, underboss of the LaTorre family.

Carlo remains leaning against the car, his posture relaxed. He removes his hands from his trouser pockets and flips them open. "I'll keep them where you can see them, if you do the same."

He eyes the guy, wishing to hell he had a weapon. "What are you doing here?" He doesn't pretend to be anything but the cop he is.

"What were you after?"

Fuck. His investigation has nothing to do with the LaTorre family, other than their association with Alexei Kaloshov. He presses his lips together, not sure how to answer.

"You after my game?"

"No." That question he could answer directly.

"Then what? One of the guys there?"

"Obviously I can't share any information about an investigation with you."

"You showed up at my game. Now I'm involved. I need to know who you're after and why."

"Why? So you can warn them?"

Carlo shakes his head. "No. So I can get rid of them. I don't need the heat."

The arrogance of the interrogation isn't lost on him nor is the implied threat of Carlo showing up within spitting distance of his family. Yet he finds a grudging respect for the man for coming straight to him for answers. The LaTorre family is still honor-bound. A throwback to a previous generation of mobsters, they've been steadily working themselves into legitimate business while the rest of organized crime has taken over the drug and flesh trade, and their practices have become more and more heinous.

"How'd you know?"

Carlo tilts his head to the side, looking him up and down. "You just didn't look right. Hair's too short. Gaze too steady. You weren't nervous enough. Guys who come in ready to spend thousands of dollars on a game are excited—already high from the adrenaline. They're sweating. Or their eyes jump around. Their fingers are wound up tight."

It's hard not to be impressed by Carlo's observational skills. He wondered how a guy in his late twenties had taken up such a position of power within the organization. This helps explain it. The guy's smart. Observant. And careful.

On a gut instinct, he violates all kinds of department policies and offers up the truth. "I wanted an introduction to Alexei Kaloshov."

"What for?"

"He runs a sex slave operation, bringing women over from Russia."

Nothing changes on Carlo's face. He can't tell whether the mobster already knew about the Russian or not.

"I can't let you into my game," he says after a moment as if he actually considered it. "You have a private phone?"

"Yeah."

Carlo lifts his hands toward his jacket then pauses and flips them, palms out again. "I'm just getting my phone." He holds his gaze and moves slowly as he opens his suit jacket, which Michael appreciates. Pulling out his phone from the inner pocket, he opens the contact screen and holds it out. "Here."

Michael takes the outstretched phone and enters his cell phone number.

"I'll let you know if I have anything for you." Carlo

takes the phone. Pushing away from the car, he starts to walk around to the driver's side.

"Carlo."

The guy turns and looks over his shoulder.

"If you ever come near my family again, I will bury you."

The mobster's lips stretch into a slow, appreciative smile. "I'd expect nothing less, detective."

# Chapter Nine

*S*ummer
Sunday dinner is sacred at the LaTorre house. I tried, my first year in college to beg out of it, but my mom laid on the guilt so thick, I soon gave up and resigned myself. Every week, my parents host a dinner for the family. My nonna and Carlo are always in attendance, and the rest of the family rotates through– Uncle Joey and Aunt Sophie, occasionally my dad's cousin Bobby and his twins, and other members of the organization.

Tonight, I arrive separately from Carlo, with our agreement not to tell anyone about the new twist in our relationship. Still, I can't account for how differently I feel about him now. I sense the moment he walks in the door because every cell in my body starts vibrating.

My body remembers the way he used me, over and over again last night. Bound spread eagle to his bed, he alternately tormented me and brought me to the brink of ecstasy. I think of the caress of his velvet tongue licking into my core, making me come so many times I thought I'd never move again. My pussy slicks now, just at the sound of his deep voice in the hall, the rich timber of his greeting to my father.

I can't decide where to look when he comes into the room. Perched on the arm of the sofa, where I was talking to my nonna, I purposely don't look over. But then, is that too obvious? Or rude? Jesus, am I blushing? I duck down to re-tie the lace of my Chucks.

"Hey Summer."

*How does he manage to pull off casual? Oh God, he's coming over.*

I jerk up, my gaze darting to his face then away as he leans in for the customary cheek kisses. How many times have I greeted him this way? Hundreds. But this time has my heart racing, my palms sweating.

He grips my elbow to pull me in, which sends a zing of excitement running through me, reminding me of his dominance. *Did he always hold my arm like that?* He gives it a squeeze before he releases it. That part is definitely new. A secret message just for me.

I don't dare look at him.

Thankfully, Uncle Joey and Aunt Sophie come in with a flurry of greetings, saving me from more awkwardness.

"Hey Summer, how's your foot?" Sophie's a massage therapist, so we always talk body stuff. "Ooh, it looks swollen, hon. Have you been dancing?"

I don't know how Sophie can tell it's swollen when

it's tucked in my shoe and sock, but she's right. The damn thing is throbbing.

"Yeah, a little." *Just not the kind of dance you're thinking of.*

"You're dancing?" I hear the sharp note of criticism in my mother's voice. Growing up, she was a total stage mom, my biggest cheerleader, but I guess she thought it was something I would quit or just do as a hobby when I went to college. She didn't like me choosing it as a college degree—said I should be using my brains, not my body. As if dance is for idiots.

I tense. "Of course. Did you think I was quitting it forever?"

The room takes on an awkward strain. I wouldn't sound so defensive if some part of me doesn't share my mother's opinion: the dance career is over. I might as well give up on the dream.

My mom puts her hands on her hips. "I just didn't know. Do you have time to get back to dance classes with your business studies?"

Of course I don't, which was exactly why my mom pushed me this way. By the time I re-emerge from my new degree, I'll be so far removed from the dance world that making a comeback will be impossible.

I sense Carlo's attention on the conversation, even though he stands casually talking to Joey, his gaze bouncing around the room with no particular interest. I'm sure he's listening, though, and I like it. The only time John ever listened to my conversation was if he was the topic.

I wonder, suddenly, how many other times Carlo paid attention to me when I thought we were just hanging out at noisy Sunday gatherings. Was this how he knew my life was a hot mess?

Thankfully, my mother disappears, returning with a platter of seasoned steaks. "Carlo or Joey, will you take these out to Al? He's warming up the grill." My mom thrusts the plate at Carlo, and a glimmer of the familiar routine returns. Men outside to grill the meat. Women talking and sipping wine around the kitchen island. I trail my mother and Sophie into the kitchen and pull out the placemats and napkins to set the table.

I pull out the plates and make a stack of twelve, carrying them into the dining room. I brought John to a few of these Sunday dinners at my mom's insistence, but my dad made them painful with his overbearing father act.

John never guessed my father was mafia, not in the entire time we were together. He was too self-absorbed, I guess. Other people close to me must know. Maggie never mentions it, but she's not obtuse. Some of my other friends have made little jokes here and there, almost like they are testing for my reaction. The girls at St. Mary's Academy knew, but some of their dads were made men, too.

I think of Carlo, my father's golden child. How different it would be to be openly dating a man like him— a guy who's part of the family business? What would dinner be like?

This line of thought doesn't really matter because this

thing with Carlo isn't permanent. It isn't a relationship. It's hot sex.

Okay, smoking hot sex.

But that's all. We're not dating. We're not going to announce an engagement around this dinner table.

He's not the kind of guy who's looking to settle down, and that's okay.

He's perfect for a rebound.

*Carlo*

Summer seemed flustered at first about being at her parents' house with me. Well, not with me. Sadly. I hate hiding that she's mine after I kept her up all night tormenting her body.

I had to leave early this morning, but I left a note with strict instructions for her to study all day and eat a good breakfast and lunch, and said I'd meet her here for Sunday dinner.

As enchanting as I find her blushes, I'm going to be in a world of trouble if Don Al notices. I suspect Donna Teresa, Al's mother, hasn't missed a thing. Obviously, if this relationship continues, I'll have to reveal it.

And I plan for it to continue.

Permanently.

But I need to figure out how to best reveal it and do it in my own way.

I wouldn't want it to come out badly. Yesterday, Vince came to drop his money by my apartment while

Summer was there, which I didn't plan for. I told her to stay in the bedroom while I met with him, but the *coglione* was peering past me like he knew I had a girl in there. Nosy fuck.

It suddenly occurs to me that if he noticed her Beamer parked on the street in front of my apartment, I'm fucked. Vince is some kind of older cousin to the don, but he's not high in the organization. He works for me, which I know bugs the hell out of him, since I'm younger and not a blood relation.

"Why don't you ever bring a date to dinner, Carlo?" Carmen probes. She's always asking about my love life. Wants me to get married and settle down.

She makes me miss my own mother.

I smile, hoping Summer doesn't take this the wrong way. "Because I don't do relationships."

Donna Teresa, Summer's nonna, smiles at this for some reason. "Waiting for the special one," she says in Italian. She's always been extra fond of me because I'm an implant from Italy like she is.

Then she flicks a glance toward her granddaughter.

If I weren't so damned intent on maintaining that Summer and I are not an item, I might celebrate the fact that the matriarch wants me for her. That she thinks I'm worthy of marrying into the Family. Maybe even that she noticed that's where my intentions lie.

But at the moment, I'm trying to cast suspicion away from Summer, hopefully without simultaneously offending her.

How in the fuck did I get myself into this position?

Joey slaps me on the back. "The harder they come, the harder they fall." He sends an adoring glance at his wife Sophie, whose belly is swollen with their first child.

"Dinner's ready." Carmen saves me from further discussion about my love life.

I end up in a seat at the dining table across from Summer, which isn't ideal because she keeps stealing glances at me. *Gesù*, it's a good thing I've had four years' practice of not staring at her because now that I've had her, my attraction has been magnified a thousand-fold. All I can think about is the way she looked spread out underneath me the night before, pulling at her restraints and moaning as I turned her apple-sized breasts rosy with a suede flogger. She was on fire for me, her beautiful pussy wet and plump, even after I took her four times.

Her ass is next. I plan to dedicate an entire week to her anal training.

As if she knows what I'm thinking, her look turns sultry. I jerk when her little socked toes caress my cock under the table. I cover the movement by adjusting my chair, scooting it closer to the table.

I should move back, out of her reach. I should frown and give her a warning look, but this sexual side of Summer makes me weak. The unexpected touch has me harder than a rock, my cock straining against my slacks.

She keeps it up, all through dessert, licking spoonfuls of tiramisu with deliberate displays of her tongue and sensual play of her lips. Her incredible, agile toes stroke along my length, tracing the lines of my cock, rolling and pressing the head against my leg.

I don't dare look at her. Lust charges through my body as I struggle to get my erection under control before the meal ends and everyone stands.

"Thank you, Carmen, this was delicious, as always." I attempt to distract myself by saying the right things.

Carmen beams at me.

Guilt rushes in. These people took me into their home. Into their family. Into their lives. I've completely debauched their daughter. Without any proper courting. Without asking permission. Without a single date. I dragged her into my bed and showed her my dirtiest forms of love-making.

Shit.

People are pushing back their chairs, stacking plates to carry to the kitchen. I need another minute. Or five.

Summer drops her foot and stands with a smirk.

I swing my focus to Al. *This man will kill you if he sees you have a boner for his little princess.* There. That helped. I take another two breaths before I push back from the table and stand.

I carry my plate to the kitchen and hand it to Summer, who looks far too smug. My beautiful little cock-tease. I'll show her the consequences of her actions the minute I get her alone. The idea of punishing her puts a smile on my face, and it must look as wicked as my thoughts because Summer's grin falters.

* * *

Twenty-three minutes.

That's how long it takes for her to emerge from the kitchen. She walks past the living room and toward the bathroom. Pulling out my phone as if I received a message, I stand and excuse myself.

I find her lingering in the hall. She must've known I'd follow. I grab her elbow and steer her into the laundry room and shut the door.

In a flash, I pin her against the wall, her wrists pressed over her head, my fingers pinching one of her nipples through her thin cotton t-shirt. Thrusting one leg between her thighs, I lean down and rumble in her ear, "Do you know what happens to girls who tease?"

She writhes against me. "What?"

I yank her skirt up to her waist and use my foot to shove her feet apart. Bringing the palm of my hand smartly up between her legs, I say, "That's not the way you answer me."

Her cheeks flush, eyes dilated and glassy.

I slap her pussy again. The gusset of her panties is already damp.

"No, sir," she yelps.

I slip my fingers inside her panties and find her swollen clit.

She gasps, bucking against me.

Another slap between her legs. My teeth nip her shoulder. "They get their pussies spanked." My voice is a low rumble, dark and devious.

She arches into me, lifting her breasts to my face. Her pussy opens to my fingers, and I shove two inside, sawing in and out. I pinch her stiffened clit and cover her mouth with my hand as she cries out.

"You may not come." I yank her panties down to her ankles and make her step out of them.

"What happens if I do?" Her voice is husky with desire.

"You'll be punished." Shoving the wad of lace and silk in her mouth, I tap open her thighs and spank her clit.

She moans and pants as I slap her juicy folds again and again. When her cries grow more desperate, I stop and release her wrists and step back.

"You do not have permission to touch yourself on the way home."

Her face clouds as she realizes I'm not going to get her off.

"Now get in your car and drive straight there," I murmur. "I want to find you naked, on your knees in the corner when I get back, or you'll be in even more trouble than you already are. Got it?" I pluck the panties out of her mouth and tuck them in my pocket.

Her eyes follow them with a pleading look.

I shake my head. "No panties for you. And no touching. I need to hear a *yes, sir*."

Her throat works as she swallows. She shoves her skirt down and straightens her shirt, looking thoroughly turned on. "Yes, sir."

I snatch her up with an arm around her waist and yank her body into mine. "I'm going to fuck you so hard you'll be sore for a week."

Her arms come around my neck, and she lifts those

sweet berry lips for a kiss, lust still swirling in her copper-flecked eyes.

I nip her lips instead. "Bad girls don't get kissed. They get fucked. *Hard*." I squeeze her ass. "Now get home and prepare yourself for me."

# Chapter Ten

*Summer*

I've never been so turned on in my life. My bare pussy lips rub together as I drive, begging to be touched, but I won't disobey Carlo, even though he'd never know the difference.

My emotions are a jumbled mess. Even though it's just a game, his mock sternness has me desperate to win my approbation. I truly feel like a sorry, chastised sex slave. If sorry, chastised slaves are also one stroke away from an orgasm.

I use the key he gave me and let myself into his apartment, breathing in his scent. I've already come to love the place. Just being here arouses me, making me feel submissive, owned.

And cared for.

That is the part I can't get over. Carlo Romano is as sweet as he is dominant. Between torturing me with his flogger, using his clever mouth and tongue between my legs, and shoving his cock into my mouth, he pushed sips of water and checked my wrist cuffs to make sure they weren't leaving marks. He watched me intently with those hazel eyes, monitoring my reactions, really seeing me.

I'm not sure anyone has ever truly seen me before. Not my parents, who want me to fit into an ideal they have for me. Certainly not John, who saw me through poop-colored glasses. Maggie knows me, but not like this. Carlo looks into my very soul...and doesn't find me lacking. His intense gazes are hard to read, but I never sense condemnation from him, never criticism.

I strip out of my clothes and eye the various corners of the bedroom. I choose the one directly to the right, so he'll have the full view of me when he walks in. Kneeling on the hard wood, I settle my bare butt on my feet, my pussy still buzzing from the spanking and my own erotic thoughts.

The key turns in the lock, and I straighten, folding my hands in my lap and staring at the corner. I listen to Carlo's footsteps as he enters the bedroom, the sound of him emptying his pockets onto the dresser, the clink of change.

"You were a very naughty girl tonight, Summer."

My pelvic floor lifts, pussy clenching. "I'm sorry, sir."

"Don't lie, *bambi*. You're not sorry."

My breasts ache, nipples tight, hardened points. Of course, he's right. I'm not sorry at all. I'm very pleased with myself.

"Come to me."

I stand, easing my weight off my swollen foot gently.

"Your foot is hurting you." He sits on the bed, his face shadowy in the lamplight.

I lift my shoulders. "A little."

"No more high heels. No more ignoring the pain. If it's swelling, you pay attention—put it up, ice it, go see your physical therapist."

I want him to stop talking about my foot and get back to the good stuff, but to avoid irritating him, I give a submissive. "Yes, sir."

His eyes narrow as if he knows I'm blowing smoke up his ass. "Okay, how about this—if I see that foot swollen and you not doing something about it, I'm going to punish you."

"Carl-o," I protest.

"I'm serious, *principessa*." He raises a stern eyebrow.

This time I do roll my eyes, which is probably not my smartest move. In a flash, I find myself over his lap with his hand slapping my ass. Considering my state of need, the pain hardly registers. I lift my butt to his hand, squirming and fighting, just to see what he'll do.

He holds me tight against his body, clamping one leg over both mine to lock me in place and slapping my upturned ass with a steady rhythm. I could orgasm from the spanking alone. My entire body buzzes, pussy quivering. Moisture leaks onto my thighs. If only I can get my fingers...

Carlo catches my hand and bends it behind my back. "Naughty angel. Did I say you could touch yourself?"

"Please, Carlo," I pant. I don't want him to stop, I want more. I need release, desperately.

"What happens if I catch you with a swollen foot?"

Despite the fact that I want him to drop the subject and move on to my pleasure, I argue with him. "That's not really fair, Carlo. I can't always drop everything and put my foot up."

He slaps the backs of my thighs, which makes me yelp. "*Bambi*, are you actually arguing with me?"

"Ow," I laugh and wriggle as he continues to spank. "No! I'm not arguing. Sorry!"

He stops spanking me, massaging my heated ass. "What happens if I catch you with a swollen foot?"

"I get punished." I sound sulky.

"I will consider the circumstances." He brushes my hair from my shoulder and smoothes it away from my face.

I give him a bit of a boo-boo lip, which seems to amuse him.

He squeezes my ass. "Stand, *cara mia*."

I push to my feet and rub my tingling cheeks.

"Hold out your hand, palm up, with your fingers spread wide."

Curious, I obey.

He scoops up something that jingles from the bed table beside him. On each of my fingertips, he lays a single dime, until I balance five coins. "Put the fingers of your other hand on top, so you're sandwiching the dimes. Good. Now turn your hands so they're vertical and lift them above your head. If you drop any of the coins, you lose your turn."

"My turn?"

His grin is devilish. "Yeah, your turn. Now, do it. When I give you an instruction, I expect obedience."

Oh, the things he says sometimes. The task is easier said than done. Keeping the pressure even on the pads of each of my fingertips takes concentration. Slowly, I stretch my arms overhead.

Carlo grips my waist and moves me back to stand in the center of the bedroom. Already my arms tremble. He walks a slow circle around me, observing my body with a heavy-lidded gaze. He's still fully dressed, while I stand naked and vulnerable.

Walking to the dresser, he picks up a little brown bottle and unscrews the cap.

I lick my lips, watching.

He puts his fingertip over the top of the bottle and inverts it. "Peppermint oil." He rubs a circle around my nipple. He repeats the action with the other one, then blows on them. They go cold—a burning cold that makes me shift my hips from side to side in frantic need.

Carlo sinks to his knees at my feet. Gripping one ankle, he pulls my feet apart. He brings his thumbs to my labia and spreads me wide.

My legs and arms tremble with the exertion of holding the position. "What are you doing?"

"Just looking, *bambi*. Looking at your beautiful pussy. You have a porn pussy, you know that?"

I almost lose the dimes as I suppress a giggle. "What's

a porn pussy?"

"This. This fucking gorgeous, shaved little pussy that drips for me right now while I watch."

It seems he'll never lose the power to make me blush. "Carlo," I choke.

He smiles up at me, showing he understands how hard I find it to stay in position. Pulling back the hood of my clitoris, he extends his tongue and gives the sensitive nubbin one quick flick.

I buck, barely managing to hold my fingertips together.

Carlo repeats the action—just a single cruel flick—enough to send spasms of sensation jolting through my core, but not enough to bring satisfaction.

"Carlo, please."

He smiles again, the leonine grin. "I like it when you beg, *principessa*."

I shiver. My elbows bend of their own accord, and I start to lower my arms.

Carlo's look turns disapproving, and my arms shoot back up toward the sky. "Do not disappoint me, *bambi*. I expect your complete obedience."

"Carlo, I can't." But I do. I don't know how we arrived at this unique relationship so suddenly, but here I am, obeying for no other reason than that he demands it.

Well, that's a lie. I obey for a multitude of reasons, and most of them revolve around the insane number of orgasms Carlo provides.

To my disappointment, he stands and walks back to the dresser, getting more peppermint oil, which he mixes with something else. When he returns, he stands behind me and grasps my throat, as if he might choke me, but his fingers are gentle. Still, the symbolic position has an effect on me. Fear—the pretend, role-playing kind—shoots through me, making my knees buckle, so the hand at my throat holds me up. Knowing that Carlo is, in fact, a dangerous man only heightens my excitement. Those same strong fingers have closed around other throats with genuine threat. They've certainly ended lives. Yet I feel completely safe in his hands, my trust in him absolute.

"Arch your back and show me your ass," he murmurs in my ear.

I tip my pelvis back. His fingers, slick with oil, find the crack of my ass. I tighten my cheeks belatedly, realizing he just applied the same stinging peppermint oil to my anus. "Carlo..."

"Are you burning for me, *bambi*?"

"Yes...please, Carlo. Please?"

"Keep begging, *cara*."

I attempt to lower my elbows again, but Carlo catches them. "Did you want the scene to end?"

My brain's turned fuzzy. Does he mean he will stop touching me if I drop the dimes? Because he promised punishment before, and that sounds perfect to me at the moment. "No-o?"

He sucks at the place where neck meets shoulder, then bites down. "You're doing very well, *amore mio*. Now stand still and get your reward."

Forcing my arms back up straight, I lock my knees.

Carlo returns to his position at my feet. Reaching

between my legs, he cradles my ass as he licks along the seam of my pussy.

I thrust my pelvis forward. "Oh..."

He seeks my back hole with one finger and massages the burning oil into the tight ring of muscle.

I'm close to spontaneous combustion; my nipples and asshole burn, my pussy pulses with desperate need. my arms ache, and the blood has run out of my hands, making it more difficult to keep the pressure on the dimes. On top of it all, lust has made me lightheaded, so I fear I might just fall over in a faint at any moment.

"Carlo, Carlo, Carlo, please."

He chuckles. "That's it, doll. Beg for it." He circles my clit with his tongue then draws the little button into his mouth, sucking hard. At the same time, he breaches my back hole with one finger.

I scream, my arms jerking, almost losing control of my precious coins. "Please, please, please. Oh God, Carlo, please."

His thumb enters my pussy, pumping in and out rapidly.

"Oh yes, oh yes, oh please." I need it faster, harder. I need more. I'm so. Damn. Close. Desperate for release. Desperate to drop my arms from their arduous task.

Carlo continues sucking, alternately pumping one finger into my ass and the thumb into my pussy.

I lose it. My scream fills the room as I lose everything —the dimes crashing down to the floor, my legs turning to jelly as my pussy spasms in wave after wave of violent release.

Carlo holds me up, still pumping his fingers, still sucking until I fall over him, my hands on his shoulders, my body limp as a rag doll.

* * *

*Carlo*

I stare down at Summer's youthful face, nestled on my shoulder in slumber. After last night, I'm completely lost. There was a reason I always wanted Summer, and it's because she was the perfect match for me.

Submissive to the core, she responds to my commands like violin strings to a bow. Her little body shakes, her pussy drips, her eyes roll back in her head at my every touch. I whipped her last night, just because I wanted to, and she took it, her arms bent behind her back, her little cries of pain making my cock harder than a rock. When I finally took her from behind, gripping her elbows and fucking her hard, she came all over my cock, her tight cunt squeezing and milking my dick until I roared my release.

Afterward, when she lay in my arms, still trembling, she looked up at me with worship and wonder on her face, and I nearly fell apart myself, wondering how I deserved such a gift.

I stroke the silky strands of her chestnut hair back from her face. My beautiful Summer. I have to figure out how to keep her. How to make this thing stick.

Despite the fact that Summer gave herself over completely in the bedroom, or maybe because she did, I worry that she isn't solid yet. She's given herself too easily, without enough caution or thought. Which either means she doesn't consider this thing to be permanent, or her emotional and mental state are still weak from her recent break-up, and she simply allowed herself to be carried off by my strong personality. Probably both.

And damn, if that doesn't make me feel guilty as hell. I didn't mean to take advantage of her. God, I only wanted to lift her—to show her how fucking beautiful I find her, to make her see what an incredible woman she is. But maybe this all just further damaged her psyche. Yes, she said she wanted to feel sexy, but I'm afraid I just traded one evil for another—objectification in a strip club for humiliation in my bedroom. Perhaps it isn't a sexual healing she needs at all but help with her busted career.

She stirs against me, and my erection lengthens and leans in her direction, already anxious for another round. Her eyes blink open, and she stares at me. I thought she might look shy, but it's the bold Summer who meets my gaze, the confident young woman I remember from when I first met her.

She shifts and climbs on top of me, straddling my hips and rubbing her bare core over my cock.

I groan.

Her lips curve into a sultry smile as her hand comes down and grasps the base of my length, and she lifts her hips, ready to impale herself on it.

"Condom," I manage to choke.

She pauses. "I'm on the pill. And I'm clean. I got checked after—"

"I'm clean," I interrupt, not wanting her to remember her fuck of a cheating ex.

"Good." She angles the head of my cock at her entrance and takes me in, her opening already slick and ready. Was she dreaming about me? The thought makes me thrust up, hard.

Her breath catches.

"Just because you're on top, doesn't mean you're in charge," I growl. Not that I don't like to see the confident, seductive side of my lover, I just want to see the effect of my words on her. It feels incredible to be inside her unsheathed, her wet heat squeezing my cock like a glove.

As expected, her eyes glaze, and she increases the rhythm of her thrusts. Her breasts bounce with the movement, the dusky rose tips stiff.

I grip her ass, yanking her over my cock.

She moans, breath turning ragged.

"Who do you belong to?"

She blinks. "You." Her voice sounds hoarse and throaty, so fucking sexy.

I'm ready to come already—she's so glorious. I bring my thumb to her clit and rub.

She shrieks and arches, her head falling back, so her long hair sweeps over my thighs, and her tits point to the ceiling. Her internal muscles spasm around my cock, and I spear her, driving up as I yank her hips down. I buck, cum shooting into her. A shudder and another long release, and she collapses on top of me, panting, her silky hair falling in a curtain across my face.

I roll out of bed and scoop her up. She weighs so

little, it's easy to carry her, and I love the way it makes me feel. Like she belongs to me. Like I'm in charge of her. Like she trusts me to be her man.

I carry her to the shower, where I wash every centimeter of her lithe body. Yeah, I could definitely get used to having Summer LaTorre staying in my place.

After we dress, I make her a veggie omelet and slide it in front of her. She brought her espresso machine over to my house, and she makes us both lattes.

"I don't usually eat breakfast." I don't like the way she squares her shoulders, as if preparing for a fight.

I watched this battle between her and her mother those first few months when I lived with them. They argued over food—over how much she ate, what she ate. Over their differing opinions on nutrition. Summer doesn't like carbs or fat although she can go to town on dessert when she loses her resolve.

"I'm not going to get into it with you over eating, *bambi*. I'll just tell you this—I love your body, and I would like it even better if there was just a little more to fill my hands. So make me happy and eat what I cook for you. It's high protein, low fat. No cheese. *Mangia*."

Her cheeks tinge with pink, and her lips part, but she doesn't say anything. *Why the blush?* She drops her head and takes a bite. "It's delicious, Carlo, thank you." *Sweet as candy*. I could definitely get used to it.

I sit across from her and fork my own omelet. "Speaking of getting into it, I want to talk to you about something."

She stiffens. "What is it?"

"What's the deal with school?"

"What do you mean?"

I shrug. "How's it going? You seem stressed but unfocused."

She stabs her egg and shoves a huge bite in her mouth, chewing slowly.

I wait.

"I hate it."

Not surprised.

"I'm probably going to get put on academic probation if I don't pull my grades up."

Conflict flits on her face—misery combined with defiance. She's always been a straight-A student, graduating at the top of her class in high school. "I don't belong in the business school."

"So quit."

Tension climbs in her shoulders. "It's not that simple, Carlo."

"It is."

She pushes her chair back and surges to her feet, fleeing me and this conversation.

"No, *bambi*. Come back, please." I catch her around the waist and haul her back against my body. My lips find her neck. "I don't mean to upset you." Plopping down in her seat, I pull her to sit on my lap. "But we're talking about this."

She blinks back tears. "This isn't any of your business."

"I'm your keeper, so everything about you is my business."

"I want out."

Ah. Her safe words. Stubborn little vixen. "No, you don't."

The defiance wavers once again, marred by a tear. She draws in a breath and exhales. "Why are you so interfering?"

I pull her face down into my neck and stroke the back of her head. "You know why, *principessa*. Because I care."

*Summer*

I lose it then, tears escaping my eyes. Everything that doesn't work in my life, that I've crammed into a pretty box and tried to wrap a bow around, comes bubbling to the surface.

He kisses my neck, rubbing circles on my back.

"*Why* do you care?" My words are muffled against his neck. Maybe what I'm really asking is–how does he care? As a friend? As my self-appointed guardian? Is this the kinky dominant talking–just part of a role he enjoys? Or is there something real between us?

He pries me off him and cradles my cheek. His gold-flecked green eyes rove over my face. His expression is soft and serious, and he opens his mouth to say something, but then seems to change his mind, closing it again.

"I just do," he says. "Now stop deflecting and tell me why you can't quit business school."

*Said the king of deflection himself.* My stomach bunches up in knots. "Can we please not talk about this?"

"Why not?"

"Because I'm going to lose my breakfast."

He strokes my cheek, and the look of sympathy brings fresh tears to my eyes. "I think you got railroaded into this by your mom, and you don't believe you can convince her this isn't the best choice."

"Right." The syllable comes out with a relieved breath. He understands. Once more, I'm surprised by how much he truly sees about me.

"But, *cara*, you're twenty-one years old. Your mother shouldn't be making major life decisions for you anymore."

The stone in my stomach gets heavier. "My parents still support me. Which means either I need to find a great job and break those ties, or I have to do what they say. And it's pretty hard to find a lucrative job without a degree and skills that don't extend beyond a ballet studio. They pay my rent and credit card bill. It's like I've had my chance to be frivolous, but the party's over, and I have to grow up and work for corporate America."

"Do you think they want you to be miserable?"

"I'm not sure that matters."

"I disagree."

It's strange and comforting to have a conversation about this with someone who actually knows my parents as well as Carlo does. Maggie and I have hashed this out a dozen times, but Maggie can't disagree with my opinions of how my family works. Hearing Carlo weigh in helps.

"I'd like you to talk to them this Sunday. I'll be there with you, if you want, to lend support."

"Carlo...I *can't*."

He regards me without expression. Like this is part of his bossman act. I'm supposed to do what he says because he's in charge of my life now. Well, that's all fine when it comes to a little spanky play, but this is my *actual life* we're talking about. It's not the same. He's overstepping.

"I'm serious," he says.

He doesn't threaten a consequence for disobedience, perhaps because this is real-life, not fetish. Even so, he shows no sign of backing down, demanding I yield to his indomitable will. It almost outweighs my anxiety over talking to my parents.

*Almost.*

"I'll try."

"What does Yoda say about *try?*"

I roll my eyes. It sometimes surprises me how much American pop-culture he's absorbed in his five years here. But I suppose they watch *Star Wars* in Italy, too.

"Sunday dinner. Alone or with me there, it needs to be done."

"Carlo." I spread my fingers, "I can't just go in there and say I want to quit. I'll need a plan to present them or something."

"Like what?"

"I should tell them what I'll do instead, though, and stripping at The Candy Store probably won't fit the bill."

"How about teaching?"

My lip curls. It's what everyone suggests, but I don't think I know enough to teach dance yet. At Tisch, I specialized in performance, not pedagogy. "I don't think I could."

"Because you're not interested or because you're afraid?"

*Very perceptive.* Who the hell is this guy anyway, and how did he manage to get in my head? I don't particularly want to answer that question, which he also seems to guess because he puts a finger under my chin to lift it.

"The truth."

"I—I just wouldn't know what I was doing."

"Right—because fifteen years of dance training hasn't prepared you well enough."

I let out a laugh. "Seventeen. Well..."

"How about if you just tell your parents you're going to look into your options for teaching, and then you can face your fears after you've cleared your plate of this business school nonsense."

I laugh again at the word *nonsense*—the exact opposite of what my mom considers it. "Okay," I say finally.

Carlo smiles. "Good girl." He helps me off his lap. "And now your eggs are cold. Remind me next time not to challenge you before you've eaten."

I laugh again, warmth infusing my chest. The guy does care. I can't deny that. And that may be what terrifies me the most. Because I could get used to this. To letting Carlo run my life. Play master to my slave. Become everything to me. And then what happens when I find out it's just another play for him?

# Chapter Eleven

C arlo

I chew the end of a cigar and look at my cards. We're at Swank, the nightclub owned by Joey LaTorre. It was half-destroyed by a bomb intended to kill all of us a few months ago. Bobby, one of the capos who owns a construction company used by the outfit to launder money, oversaw the rebuilding, and had his crews working round the clock, so our evening head-quarters was restored in a matter of weeks.

We resumed our weekly game immediately–a *fuck you* to the Matrangas for trying to take us down. And Sammy. The fucker who betrayed us. Wish I'd been the one to end him. I would've made it a long and drawn-out affair. I've got a mean streak I don't mind flexing for Family business.

I don't love cigars, but it's part of the male bonding. Al loves them, and this is the way we commune with him. Joey's here, a changed man since the explosion. Or maybe it's since Sophie. But things shifted between him and Al, too. He's taken a step back from the day-to-day operations of the outfit. He sticks to numbers and legit business enterprises. I've taken a step forward with the most dangerous activities.

The atmosphere of this game was night and day different from my high-stakes game. That one is business: this is pleasure. Loud voices fill the room, men talking with their hands, boasting and bragging, razzing each other in a good-natured way.

"So, Carlo, you got a new girlfriend?"

Fucking Vince.

Some heads swivel in my direction.

"No."

"No? Really? I thought you had a girl there when I stopped by Saturday." The guy glances at the don, and I want to kill him.

I work hard not to visibly stiffen. Fuck. I hope Vince didn't figure out I had Summer over at my place.

I want to say, "Just a piece of ass," to shut him up, but if Vince thinks it was Summer, no way I'm going to disrespect her that way.

Al eyes me, probably picking up my discomfort. The guy's good at reading people. "Do you have a new girlfriend?"

"No." I need to tread carefully here. If—when—it comes out I'm dating Summer, I don't want to be guilty of any lies. "I've been seeing someone. Not officially a girlfriend yet, but I'm working on it."

Al's face breaks into a broad smile, and guilt makes

me queasy. "So she's girlfriend material? It's about time you made a real connection. You'd be more respectable if you had a woman."

*Yeah, especially if that woman is the don's daughter.* Unless the don objects, in which case I'm a dead man, as the saying goes. Funny how my original attraction to Summer was the very fact that she was the mafia princess, and now it's what gives me nightmares. It's not about marrying into the family anymore. That was a foolish ambition of my early years. No, now it's just about Summer. The woman who's captured everything for me.

The culture of *La Famiglia* is old-fashioned. The woman you marry isn't the one you fuck like a whore. You keep the depravity out of the family house. I suppose that idea was bred into me, and yet discovering that the pure, wholesome angel I set my sights on marrying is also willing to submit to my depravity sent my worlds colliding. But in a good way. A perfect way. I don't really objectify women the way the guys around me do. To me, Summer's everything—all I can see, all I will ever need.

I want to claim her for real—not in my bed, but as my wife, as my forever-girl. But it's far too soon. She's still mixed up and on the rebound. And I haven't figured out how to play things with her parents. It's been less than two weeks since I found her stripping at The Candy Store. This situation requires patience, which has never been my strong suit.

I eye Joey, Al's younger brother. He serves as a resource—an investment broker, an advisor. He might have some advice about how to handle this situation with Summer.

I hang around late, even though the thought of Summer at home in my bed makes me crazy. The guys all get up around the same time to go, and I walk out to the club with them, hanging back without being obvious about it.

"Hey I gotta show you something if you can stay for a sec." Joey lifts his chin at me.

"Sure thing." Lucky break. I wander back to his office and wait. When he comes, I ask, "What's up?"

"Nothing, I got the feeling you wanted to talk to me."

Smart fuck. And I thought I was perfectly subtle. I'll have to watch myself in the future.

"You were hanging back at the end there. What's up?"

Well, now I have no choice but to come out with it now. "Summer's the girl I'm dating."

Joey lifts a brow. "My niece, Summer." He doesn't say it like a question. More like I'm in deep shit.

"Yeah." Damn, my heart is hammering. Jesus.

I lost my entire family four years ago.

The LaTorres are all I have now. I didn't realize how afraid I am of losing my place here. But who am I kidding? I might lose more than my place if I truly offend the don. I could lose everything–including my life.

Joey folds his arms across his chest. "Do you have a death wish?"

A flare of irritation runs through me. I may respect the don, but I'm also worthy of his daughter. Besides, there's no backing out now. I jumped in with both feet. To reverse directions now would hurt Summer. And beyond that, I have no intention of giving her up. My lips flatten. "Why?" I ask, even though I know exactly why.

Joey blows out his breath. "He'll kill you."

My throat tightens. My hands turn cold. "Literally?"

Joey tips his head to the side, considering. "Nah. At least, I don't think so. Not unless you hurt her. But Christ, why'd you have to pick her?"

The misery on my face must've been apparent because Joey's brows rise, and he walks forward and drops a hand on my shoulder. "Wow, you got it bad, don't you?"

The words open up some crack that's always been inside me. Or at least since the day I landed in the LaTorre house four years ago. Emotion pours out, gushes over me, fogs my brain. For some stupid reason, the memory of standing outside my great-uncle's house four years ago, stripped of my family, at a loss for how to move forward flashes through my mind, making the scar on my ear burn.

I reach up and rubbed it. "Yeah," I manage to answer.

Joey paces around the room, rubbing his forehead. "Al loves you like a son. Or a brother." His smile is rueful as if he regrets letting Al down by taking a step back from running of the organization. "My honest opinion? I think he'll be pissed at first but get over it—*if* she really wants to be with you."

The suggestion that she might not grates but only because I'm not sure myself. Does she want this, or have I just foisted it on her when she was at her weakest? Would she wake up in three weeks or a month and say she's had enough?

"If you're not sure yet if this is a real thing, I wouldn't say anything. Not when things are new and tenuous. You'll want to present it as a united front, I think. He loves you both, he's going to want what makes you both happy, and if that's each other, he might be able to swallow it."

Some of the tension in my stomach eases hearing Joey share the same views I do on holding off.

"As much as Carmen loves you, I think she'll fight it. She's like Sophie's mom—she doesn't necessarily want her daughter to make the same choice she did about marrying into *la famiglia*. I think she wants some nice WASP-y city councilman for Summer, something as far from you and me as it gets."

I shove my hands in my pockets and try not to scowl. I suppose I knew this obstacle existed, too. In some ways, it's a harder problem to overcome than Al's wrath.

Joey shrugs. "So you just persist."

"Is that how you won over Sophie?"

"Yeah." He grins. "You gotta fight for the woman you love, even if she isn't sure."

I extend my hand, and Joey grasps it, pulling me into a man-hug, thumping my back. "*Grazie molte.*"

"Yeah, anytime." He pulls away. "But you know, if you hurt that girl, I'll kill you, too."

I smile. "I have no doubt of that. 'Night, Joey." Walking to the door, I consider Joey's advice. Fighting for

Summer makes sense in theory, but in reality, she's fragile right now. I've already come on way too strong. If I were a better man, I'd give her a lot more space right now.

But hell. I shove my hands back in my pockets. I'm not a better man, am I?

* * *

*Summer*

I sit in my car in front of Northeast Ballet Academy, my childhood dance studio. Little girls in buns and pink tights walk in holding their mothers' hands and carrying their net bags with ballet shoes. That was me at age three. I trained here in ballet up through high school.

Ana Teasedale, the owner, was my first employer, hiring me at age thirteen to help as a student assistant with the tiny tots.

At age fourteen, my mom started driving me into New York City to take master classes at other studios, but I kept it from Ana, fearing she'd see it as a betrayal.

At age seventeen, I won an apprenticeship with Joffrey Ballet, and I had to drop out of the Northeast Nutcracker performance. Ana was pissed. Understandably. She was blindsided by the whole thing and had to put a lesser performer in the lead to take my place.

At the time, I told myself she was threatened by my success. Now, with a little more perspective, I can see that I didn't handle things well. I kept my aspirations to move on from Northeast a secret and then abruptly bailed on her.

But the Joffrey was a dream come true. I was selected the year Carlo arrived. I thought I was such a big shot. I left Northeast Ballet and didn't look back—never stopped in for a visit or sent a Christmas card or anything.

I consider going in to say hello, but now, as I sit here watching the rush of students, I realize it's a bad time. Ana will be busy in the office if she isn't in one of the studios, and I wouldn't have time to...well, I owe her an apology for leaving and never coming back until now. And for my arrogance in just writing off everything she taught me. In retrospect, the technique and discipline I learned here has served me very well. I never had to unlearn any bad habits, the way some dancers do. Hell, I never would've made it into the apprenticeship program if it hadn't been for Northeast.

Putting the car into drive, I pull out and head to Carlo's apartment. I could start with an email to Ana. It's a chicken-shit approach, but at least I'd have time to think about what to say and how to say it. I've never been good at dealing with people on the fly.

It's too bad—I had this little fantasy about telling Carlo I followed his advice and started teaching. I wonder how he would reward me? Would it still involve me naked and merciless under his hands.

I smile to myself, my core tightening at the idea.

Of course, telling Carlo would mean confessing I went somewhere besides class without his permission. Not that I mind a little punishment at his hands.

I've never had so much attention from a man in my life. He notes what I eat, what I don't eat. How much I study, how much I sleep. Wednesday, when I woke up after him being out late playing poker, I found a dozen pink roses in a vase with a note that just said, "Make sure you eat a good breakfast, *principessa*."

So I ate breakfast. In fact, I've eased back on my obsessive monitoring of food. If I'm brutally honest with myself, I'll admit that I've used food in the past year or two—or the withholding of food—as self-punishment. Punishment for not being able to keep John's attention. Or for ruining my dance career. Or not being perfect.

Maybe now that Carlo's taken over my punishments—and made them pleasurable—I can let myself eat. He doesn't make me feel bad about myself. On the contrary, I'm starting to feel alive again. Sexy. He makes me feel beautiful when he devours me with his gaze or demands sex from me at all times of the day. Or devotes hours to the delicious torture of my body.

But he also demands something deeper from me. A part of me I didn't know existed. Or I did, but hated. My real self, complete with fears and insecurities. Hopes and dreams.

This morning, he rolled me over and kissed down my back then examined how my ass had survived the play from the night before.

"Are you still sore, *cara*?"

"Only my pride."

"Baby girl, you don't have any pride. At least, not with me. I require you to be fully bared. Completely vulnerable."

I went still.

As if he knew the fear his words inspired, he said, "I promise I won't let you fall." He stroked his hand over my ass. "That, my sweet, is what will allow you to be your most sexual self. You'll give me everything because I demand it, and you'll have no choice."

I almost came just from those words, my core turning molten. Carlo had put me on my knees and fucked me from behind until I screamed my release. Afterward, he kissed me with so much passion, I was ready to hop on his cock all over again.

I press the gas pedal down, suddenly in a hurry to get to his place, hoping he's there.

He is.

I push the door open to find him on the sofa, a sexy smirk on his face as if he was waiting for me. Mother of God, he takes my breath away. Those dark-lashed green eyes, the curling dark locks falling over his forehead, the shadow of stubble on his jaw. He's debonair and drop-dead gorgeous. He carries a gun and engages in dangerous unknown business affairs that probably fall outside the law, and that only heightens his dangerous appeal.

"I have something for you, *bambina*."

"You do?"

"Yes. A present. It's in the bedroom. Go and see."

I laugh softly, thinking for sure it's some kind of sex toy or lingerie. Something kinky, so he can do more freaky things to my body. I run to the bedroom and push open the closed door. Nothing was on the bed. Nor the dresser.

I look around.

A little sound comes from under the bed and a tiny, fluffy black and white kitten emerges, stretching and trotting toward me, already purring.

"Oh my God," I squeal, dropping to my knees to catch the little thing.

A second one emerges from the bed. I laugh. "Another one! How many are there?"

"Just the two, *cara*. Do you like them?"

I scoop them both up and hold them against my chest, rubbing my face in their soft fur. One is black with a white nose and paws, the second is white with black on its back, tail and ears. "They're adorable." I rush back into the living room. "I can't believe you bought me kittens."

He smiles indulgently. "They're almost as cute as you are. But not quite."

I walk around the sofa and drop into his lap, nuzzling into him as I hold the purring kittens.

"What will you name them?"

"Hmm. Oreo? No–I've got it! This one is Cookies" –I hold up the black one– "and this one is Cream." I kiss the white one.

"Love it."

He bought me kittens. It isn't a big gift. Or showy. But so thoughtful. He listens to me. He heard when I said I've always wanted a cat. He paid attention.

If I could purr, I would. "Thank you, Carlo." The words *I love you* rise to my lips, but I bite them back in time.

Crap, I can't be falling in love. This is just sex. Just.

Sex. Except it isn't. It's so much more than sex. Hell, it's more than most people's marriages.

Carlo is my keeper, my master. And that scares the hell out of me because I want this forever, and I heard what Carlo said at my parents' house.

He doesn't do relationships.

# Chapter Twelve

*arlo*

C The warehouse for Friday's game sits near the docks, an old meat-packing plant in the twenties, now a chop-shop for stolen vehicles. The space has been transformed, as usual, with the addition of Christmas lights twinkling from the rafters—Sonny's idea.

The Russian shows up smelling of vodka and sex. His designer shirt is wrinkled as if he slept or fucked in it.

I don't usually get into my customers' business, but finding out the guy is a sex trafficker got under my skin. I suppose I should've known. The Russian *mafiya* run the majority of the drug business in New Jersey, particularly the ecstasy trade, but there been rumors of sex slaves. While I have no problem with prostitution, slavery is something altogether different. You don't force women to have sex. Not unless It's pre-negotiated, and they like that sort of thing, of course—and I've had a few of those.

No, the idea of women or girls being kidnapped and sold into sexual slavery makes my blood boil. It makes me want to put a cap in the Russian bastard's cruel face.

So I wouldn't mind helping the undercover detective with his investigation. But I can't let him into my game. If word got out a cop sat at my table, I'd lose every customer I have, not to mention all my street cred. No, I won't be the way Detective Bailey gets an introduction to Alexei, but I'll keep my eyes and ears open to see if another opportunity arises.

Sonny takes the guy's money and pushes a pile of chips over to him. Only five players showed up tonight— the Russian and his cohort, two Wall Street businessmen and the Cuban. The low turnout doesn't bother me. Sometimes more money is to be had with small games, anyway. Guys feel luckier, are less likely to fold.

We give it another five minutes, and then I signal to Sonny to start dealing. I don't play myself, just observe, along with Vince. Using four decks to prevent any card counting, Sonny deals the first hand. One of the Wall Street guys takes the pot. The Russian takes the next hand. Then the Wall Street again. By the end of the night, the Russian has been cleaned out of chips. He turns to me. "Spot me another three thousand. You know I'm good for it."

Spotting money and collecting with interest is an easy gig, and one the Family has been involved with for as long as there's been organized crime. But collecting from another mobster, particularly a Russian, could be problematic. Maybe I just want to see the guy lose again, or maybe I want him beholden, but for whatever reason, against my better judgement, I nod at Sonny, who pushes the chips across the table.

And of course, as always happens when a man is desperate and pushed beyond his means, Alexei loses it all in the very next round.

He shoves back from the table, his pale face flushed.

When he starts to stalk out without a word, I call him back, my tone cool and professional. "We need to discuss the terms of repayment, Mr. Kaloshov." I go extra polite, not trusting the man's rage.

Alexei lets out a flurry of Russian, which sounds mostly like swearing. "I have payment for you right here." His accent is thick with anger. "It's in my trunk. A woman. Sex slave. Worth more than three thousand on the black market."

Mr. Big, the fake name of the Wall Street businessman who took most of the winnings looks up, cool and calculating. "Where is she? Let me see her—is she Russian? Blonde?"

*Stronzo.*

Alexei turns to him and lifts his chin. "Blue-eyed blonde. Big tits. Very pretty. You'll like her."

"Bring her in."

I don't know when the fuck I lost control of arrangements, but I'm sure as hell not going to let this exchange go down. I trail Alexei to the door and order two of my soldiers to follow him to the car as I watch from the door.

Alexei pops the trunk to the car and pulls out a girl in nothing but a teddy and thong. Her feet are bare. She isn't tied up, but when he sets her on her feet, she wobbles, as if she's been drugged. Alexei half-leads, half-drags her back to the warehouse.

She appears naturally fair, but her hair has been bleached platinum blond. She smells like cheap, fruity perfume.

"Here she is." Alexei presents her to Mr. Big. He lifts the hem of her teddy up to expose her tits, not that much was left to the imagination to begin with. "See? Very sexy. She's yours to keep. You can do anything you like with her. A lifetime of satisfaction."

"I'll take the girl." I ignore the looks of surprise on Sonny and Vince's faces. No girl is getting sold into slavery on my watch—I don't care if it costs me three grand.

"No, I'll take her." Mr. Big steps forward and grips her arm possessively.

My lips thin and eyes deaden. I'm sure I look as lethal as the Russian, and I am. *"She's mine.* Vince, pay him out."

Vince has already been packing bundles of cash into a briefcase for the guy, and he resumes his work, asking Sonny to double-check the count before rotating the case for Mr. Big.

Big appears burned up over me claiming the girl, but he can't do anything about it. It's my show. The players' weapons have been confiscated. Only my men and I are armed.

He counts his cash and walks out, still looking back at the girl as if he can't stand letting her go.

Alexei turns to the girl and says something to her in Russian.

Her eyes are glazed and unfocused, but she still cringes at the sound of his voice. He slaps her on the ass and the girl jumps. That's when I notice her back and legs are lined with brutal belt-marks. Her forearms are tracked with needle-marks. They've beaten her and kept her high on drugs to ensure her cooperation.

I should murder Alexei for sport. But this guy is Russian *mafiya*. I can't take action that would start a war between the Russians without the don's approval.

"Enjoy." Alexei tries to give her another slap, but I catch his wrist.

"Mine now."

He must catch the murder in my gaze because he sobers, significantly. There's a charged breath, during which I'm sure he's considering challenging me then realizes he's greatly outnumbered. He shrugs. "Fine."

I watch him leave with a death glare on his back, then guide the girl to sit in a chair and press a bottle of water from the portable bar in her hand.

She looks at it for a long moment, as if she's never seen one before, but then brings it to her cracked lips with a shaking hand. The green-yellow hue of an old bruise stands out on her cheekbone.

When the other players depart, Vince turns to me. "What the fuck are you going to do with her? I mean, really kid?"

I stay cool, but murder's already in my blood. "Call me *kid* again, and I'll knock your fucking teeth out and shove them up your ass." I'm the guy's boss, whether I'm twenty years younger than he is or not. I deserve a little respect.

Vince's lip curls, but he shrugs. "Sorry, Carlo. No offense intended."

"I'm not going to keep the girl, *coglione*. Do you two think I'm going to sit around and let some girl get sold into a lifetime of slavery at *my* game? What the hell is wrong with you? Women don't sign up for this shit. She's been kidnapped and repeatedly raped and obviously knocked around."

Vince throws her a doubtful glance. "She looks like a junkie."

"No shit." I throw my hands in the air. "That's how they keep her pliant."

Vince and Sonny both sober, either pretending to understand or actually getting it now. "So what are you going to do with her?" Sonny asks.

I pick up my phone and scroll through for the cop's phone number. "I'm going to call that cop who showed up at the game last week. This is what he's trying to bust up."

"We'll take care of things here, if you want to take care of the girl." Sonny's a good right-hand man. Loyal, eager-to-please. Not always the best decision-maker, but that might come with time.

"Thank you." I pick up the briefcase of money and pay out the two guys, leaving a stack of money for them to pay out the rest of the crew for the night.

Grasping the girl's elbow, I help her to her feet.

"Okay, hon, let's get you out of here. Do you speak English?"

She swings her unfocused gaze to my face and stumbles as I lead her to the door, looking terrified. She might not speak English, and she might be drugged, but she understands she's been sold.

And I have no way to tell her she's safe.

* * *

An hour later, after calling the detective and taking the girl to the police department, I get home. I'm certain Summer will be asleep–it's one in the morning.

But she waited up. She greets me with far more enthusiasm than I deserve.

I disentangle her arms from around my neck and give her a perfunctory kiss. "Go to bed, *bambina*. I'll be in soon."

She's disappointed, but I feel too dirty to touch her. And not the kind of soil a shower can wash off. What I saw tonight–human trafficking–makes me sick.

It grinds up against my moral codes. I've murdered. I use intimidation, violence, and threats to get my way on a fairly regular basis. I operate in a world of crime. Always have. I was born into this life. Raised in it. I have nerves of steel when it comes to most things.

I don't know why this shit bothered me so much.

Actually, I do.

It's too close to the games I play at in bed. The non-consensual version.

That girl had been whipped. Used.

What happened to her was wrong on every level. Yet those are the exact scenes and scenarios I love to enact in my own bedroom. With my willing partners.

I'm a sick fuck, and I've taken the don's daughter–the princess of the mafia–into my warped world. I've trained her as a submissive. Treated her like a pretend sex slave.

It's so wrong.

I turn on the television, unable to face the sweet girl I've corrupted.

When I fall asleep, my dreams are soaked in guilt.

*I've been on a killing rampage, taking down a rival family back in Italy. I gun down the last one and step over him to take the girl he was keeping prisoner. It's the Russian girl. I put her in my car without untying her, and then she turns into Summer. Tied up. At my mercy. Begging for an orgasm as I drive the car. But then we're hit from behind. Glass shatters. Metal crunches.*

*Gunshots riddle the car with holes. I hold Summer's head down to keep her safe.*

*Mario looks through the shattered window. He's holding a gun. "You shouldn't have taken the girl."*

*"I know," I say, but I'm unwilling to give her up. Unwilling to make it right by giving Summer to Mario or returning her where she belongs.*

*He points the gun at my temple. "Then you know what I have to do."*

# Chapter Thirteen

*ummer*

S     I wake before Carlo and get in the shower.

It might be time to end this little fling with him. I suspect he's getting bored, and I'd rather be the one to end things first. Salvage my pride and all that.

For the first time since I moved in a week ago, he wasn't interested in sex last night. He came home from whatever work he was doing last night and seemed shut down.

I had stayed up for him, and I threw my arms around his neck, offering up a kiss, but he gave me a perfunctory peck and disentangled himself from me.

"Is everything okay?"

"It's fine, *Bambi*. Go to bed, I'll be in in a minute."

I went to the bedroom and stripped down to my panties, waiting, but he never came in. Instead, I heard the television go on.

It's not like we have to have sex every night. He might

be tired. Or stressed out. Just because he spent hours giving me mind-blowing orgasms the rest of the week doesn't mean he always will.

But it hurt my feelings way more than it should have, which is why I think I should probably end things.

Carlo's up and dressed when I get out of the shower. "*Buongiorno.*" He cups my nape and kisses me in that masterful way he has that makes my knees go weak. I try to stay strong, breezing past him and getting dressed.

He leans against the doorframe, hands in his pockets, watching me. "Sorry I was a dud last night. Can I take you to breakfast, *principessa?*"

I shrug into a cute dress. Maybe I was being hasty. "Yeah. That'd be nice."

I lace up a pair of high-top Chucks and enjoy Carlo's appreciative sweep of my bare legs.

He leads me out to his Mercedes and opens the door for me. When I settle in the passenger seat the scent of cheap perfume assaults my senses. My head spins as Carlo gets in and starts driving. With a sick lurch, the pieces of the puzzle rearrange themselves and fall into place. He didn't want to have sex last night because he'd already had it.

I want to puke.

He's no different from John or any other cheating bastard. Not that we ever had a discussion about exclusivity, but Mother of God, I'm staying at his apartment!

"Pull over." I grip the door handle.

"What? Why?"

"Pull over the car, right now." I start to open the car door, and he swerves to the curb.

"Summer, what—?"

I jump out before the car stops rolling, not shutting the door behind me.

I hear the slam of a door and heavy footsteps behind me as Carlo flies out in hot pursuit. Horns honk behind his SUV.

"Summer, what in the hell is going on?" He jogs to keep up with me, catching my elbow.

I shake him off, baring my teeth. "Don't touch me."

He continues jogging beside me, holding his palms up. "I'm not touching. Just tell me what's going on."

I cock my arm and slap his face as hard as I can, tears spilling from my eyes.

Before I turn away, I see deep concern on his face. But then, if he's a player, he'd be very good at playing, wouldn't he?

He catches me around the waist and pulls my back against his front.

I struggle against his hold, but his forearm is like steel.

"Hey." His voice is soft in my ear. "I'm not going to hurt you, but I'm sure as hell not going to let you run away without at least telling me why you're upset."

"Who was she?" I demand.

Carlo goes still, confirming my worst fears.

"Oh God," I croak.

"No, baby, no. You've got it all wrong. Something happened last night, and I will tell you all about it. But not out here. At home. Or at least in the car."

"I'm not getting in that car with you."

"Summer, please. The truth will not hurt you, I swear. I would never cheat on you. Not ever."

My breath rasps in my chest. *Not ever.*

The place inside my solar plexus that's vibrating like a frantic moth caught in a lampshade eases. He *does* consider us exclusive, then.

And he swears he would never cheat. It's a misunderstanding. Or am I being gaslit?

No, Carlo has honor. Or at least I thought he did. But then again, how much did I know about him?

"Your car smells like perfume."

Carlo blows out his breath. "I'm sure it does. And there's an explanation. Do you want to hear it?"

I do, but I also want to hold my ground. This isn't the time to let Carlo boss me around.

"She's a Russian sex slave being held against her will. I don't know her name. I took her somewhere safe. Now, can we please get in the car? I really don't want to be talking about this out here."

I slump back against his body, all the fight leaving me. My legs wobble.

"I'm sorry you thought something happened, *bambina,* but I'm not that guy. I'm not going to fuck around on you. Not ever."

He turns me around to face him. "Look at me." Cradling my face in both hands he locks eyes with me. "You're my girl. I'm not going to do anything to mess that up."

"I'm sorry. I shouldn't have freaked out. It's just that John–"

Carlo's face contorts with irritation. "I'm nothing like John."

"I know. I'm sorry." I sniff as he thumbs away my tears.

"Get in the car, and I'll explain everything—if you want me to, that is."

"Yes. I'm sorry. I need to hear it." I let him lead me back to the car, where my door still stands ajar. I climb in and let him shut the door.

When he gets behind the wheel, he says, "I didn't do anything illegal, so telling you won't make you an accessory. Even so, the less you know, the safer you are."

"I need to know."

"I run a gambling table every Friday night. Okay, that part's not legal. It's high stakes. One of my customers is Russian *mafiya*. He borrowed funds last night and offered this girl up to settle his debt."

I gape at him, trying to comprehend what he's telling me. "So...you ended up with a Russian sex slave?"

"Right."

A sick feeling forms in my stomach. I'm not sure I want to hear the rest of the story. I really have no idea what kind of business my father and Carlo run. I know they're mafia. I know I'm not supposed to know any of it. Would they have use for such a girl? Carlo said the truth wouldn't hurt me, but that just means he hasn't used the poor woman himself.

"A cop came by a few weeks ago, trying to get in on

my game. When I questioned him, he told me he was after this Russian, to break open the slave ring. So I called him. Brought her to a meeting place, so she could be questioned and taken care of."

"Oh my God. That poor girl." Fresh tears smart my eyes.

I go soft and moony for Carlo. He was a hero. Protecting the weak. Getting that woman to safety. He has so much more honor than I gave him credit for.

My role as mafia princess has always been to turn a blind eye, ask nothing, see nothing. Accept the wealth that came from my father's dealings.

Getting involved with Carlo makes me question whether I can continue doing so for the rest of my life. To willingly choose to go on, knowing he deals in the shadowy side of business. Hearing he's as much a hero in his business dealings as he is with me comes as a relief.

I shake my head. "I'm sorry I assumed the worst. It's just— you didn't want to have sex with me when you came home last night. And then when I smelled the perfume..."

"I know. I'm sorry." He rubs his forehead. "Summer, this girl was in bad shape. She had track marks running up both arms, like they kept her constantly drugged, and..." He breaks off, looking sickened.

"What?" My voice comes out as no more than a croak.

He presses his lips together, his nostrils flaring.

"Carlo, what?"

He shakes his head. "She was barely dressed. She had

on this little teddy and a G-string, and her back and ass were all marked up."

My stomach twists as I suddenly understand where his thoughts are headed. He's comparing what we do with the abuse this woman endured.

"Carlo, that's different."

He starts the car and pulls out into traffic, as if he doesn't want to talk about it anymore.

"Carlo, are you telling me you couldn't have sex with me last night because..." I struggled for the right words. "We're different. You know that, right?"

A furrow deepens between his brows as he watches the traffic with more intent than necessary.

"Carlo?"

He rubs the back of his neck, still not looking at me.

"You don't think—" I give an exasperated sigh. "Carlo, she also had sex forced on her, do you think every guy who has sex is wrong, too?"

Carlo's eyebrows shoot up, and he finally glances over. Something in the set of his shoulders eases. "God, it just...disturbed me."

"Well, of course it did. It disturbs me just hearing about it." I reach out and touch his knee. "Please tell me you're not going to shut off your dominance now because you saw an example of abuse."

He parks on the street in front of a popular breakfast joint then turns to look at me. His expression is still troubled, but he leans forward and kisses my forehead. "Thanks, *principessa*."

"I'm sorry, I overreacted. I'm embarrassed now."

He shrugs. "All good. You were upset. I can take a punch or two. You have bad history that way, so you jumped to a conclusion. But I meant it when I said I'm not that guy. Do you believe me?"

I want to. So badly. I want to trust this guy with my whole heart. Why is it so terrifying? But he's waiting for an answer, so I nod.

"Please don't run off again without giving me a chance to explain myself. And for fuck's sake, don't open the door on a moving car. You scared the shit out of me."

"I'm sorry." I squeeze his hand, grateful for the man who already seems to hold my entire world together. "Are you going to punish me?"

His eyes crinkle at my obvious attempt to push him back into his dominant role. "I guess I'd better."

He pushes open the door and meets me on the side-walk, taking my hand. "What did I tell you would happen if you slapped me again?"

My pulse kicks up another notch, heat pooling between my legs. "You said you'd put a plug in my ass and stand me in a corner."

A smile twists on his lips. "You paid attention." He sounds pleased.

With that thrilling consequence hanging over me, I have no idea how I'll make it through breakfast, but Carlo's in a rare, sharing mood, so I use it to probe into his past.

After we've ordered our food, I ask, "Do you miss your family back home?"

Carlo nods. "I miss...nothing and everything. I mean,

I'm happy here. This is my home now. But my mother probably doesn't know I'm alive or dead."

I work to swallow, realizing the enormity of that. How I'd ache to see my mom if I had to stay in hiding.

"Your poor mom."

He nods. "Every year on her birthday I send flowers." He shrugs. "I guess I hope she knows they're from me. That I'm alive. But I can't make contact otherwise."

"So no contact with anyone? No one knows you're alive?"

"My great aunt and uncle know. They're the ones who connected me with your dad. I'm still in the business with my uncle–importing grappa."

"Do you ever...want revenge?" I know I shouldn't ask incriminating questions, but this is Carlo's very heart and soul. His own brother tried to kill him.

I can't imagine how that would affect a person.

He hesitates. His lips thin.

"No." It comes out like an exhale. "I never have." He shrugs. "I'm ruthless as hell when it comes to business decisions, but..." he trails off and shakes his head.

I see an ocean of pain in his expression.

My vision blurs, and I reach for his hand across the table.

"It's different when you love someone. Mario saved my life a dozen times. He could be a cocksucker, but he's still my brother. You know?"

I don't have any siblings, but I can imagine. "Is he your only brother?"

Carlo shakes his head. "No. I'm the youngest of five."

"Is there any possibility you could reconcile? If he knew you didn't want him dead and don't want to usurp him?"

Carlo drains his espresso cup. "I don't know. Not sure I'd even want that."

"Because you haven't forgiven him?"

Carlo gives a slow nod. "Right." A glimmer of a sad smile plays around his lips. "I don't want to kill him, but I haven't forgiven him. A purgatory of sorts."

"Here's the thing about forgiveness. Withholding it only costs you. It makes no difference to the person you're mad at." I know this because I've been working on forgiving John. I know hanging onto the grudge only harms me.

I'm not there yet, but I know it's true.

"But you're ready when you're ready," I say, realizing the same will be true for me.

Carlo considers me. "I'll think about it. Thank you." He holds my gaze with his steady green one. "You're a treasure."

*Carlo*

"Over my lap, *principessa*."

That night, I get Summer naked for her punishment. I'm fully clothed, the way I like it for a power exchange scene.

I felt lighter after our discussion over brunch. I don't talk about Mario with anyone, so having Summer share the burden and my secret changed things for me. I let her in.

She's the first person I've really let in since I came to this country. The only one I've revealed this vulnerability to.

It's easy when she offers up her vulnerability to me every minute of the day.

I need to figure out how to talk to Al about this. Summer is fully mine—she's given herself to me, and I'm not letting her go.

She folds herself over my lap now. I haven't touched her there yet, but her pussy already glistens with dew simply from the act of baring herself for me.

I stroke the curves of her muscular ass, down her long, shapely thighs. Fucking gorgeous. Drawing my hand back, I land a smack on the lower portion of her right cheek.

She holds still for me.

Such a perfect submissive. I love how soft and sweet she goes for me. The way she gives me moony looks from under those lashes.

I smack the other cheek, then rub the sting away. Warming her up slowly, I slap and stroke until her ass turns an enchanting shade of blush. Only then do I increase the intensity, spanking her harder and picking up the tempo.

She clenches her ass muscles and makes little gasping noises that make my already stiffened cock go rock hard. The gasps turn into grunts and little cries. I'm not giving her time to assimilate the pain, so it quickly overwhelms her senses. Sure enough, her hand comes flailing back, trying to cover. I catch her wrist and pin it behind her back.

Summer looks over her shoulder. "Carlo, I'm sorry!"

"I know. But you were a naughty girl, *tesoro mio*, and now your ass must pay the price."

She wriggles as if trying to dodge my hand. "Please!"

I have no intention of stopping because the wriggling and the begging is just part of the game. I could spank her to tears, and she'd still be dripping wet for me. Summer's wired as a true submissive, her masochism a complement or maybe a result of her dance career.

She's a perfect complement to me. Satisfaction surges with each crack of flesh against flesh, the sting of my palm and the bounce of her cheeks fueling my lust.

I stop and caress her heated skin. Smooth the hair away from her face.

She looks back at me, a question on her face.

Leaning over, I kiss her temple and some of the tension leaves her body. She could probably take any amount of pain with enough positive encouragement.

"Reach back and pull open your naughty cheeks." My voice sounds deep and rough.

"What?"

I lightly slap the back of her legs, right and left. "You heard me, beautiful. Therefore, the only correct answer is *yes, sir*." I pop her twice more when she still doesn't move.

"Yes, sir!" She makes a whimpering sound but

reaches back and grips her reddened cheeks, gingerly pulling them open.

"Good girl." I pick up the lube I placed on the table beside the sofa and squeeze a dollop out onto her little rosette.

She jumps.

Picking up the stainless-steel plug, I rub the rounded tip at her pussy's entrance. She spreads her thighs and lifts her ass. "You're so wet. You'd like me to fuck your pussy with this plug, wouldn't you?" I do just that, pushing the large object into her dripping canal.

She humps my lap, trying to get more.

Abruptly, I pull it out and position it at her back hole. "When you're naughty, Summer, you'll experience my displeasure. I'll make your ass red and sore before I take it with my cock."

"Oh God," she warbles, sounding both fearful and turned on.

Her inner thighs tremble, and her breath comes in little pants.

"Take it, *principessa*." I push past her tight ring of muscles, gaining entrance.

"Oh...whew. Uhn."

I love her noises. Easing the plug in further, I press it in and retreat, gradually stretching her tight hole until I work the widest part of the plug into her, and it seats.

"Ahhh."

"That's right, *bambina*. Your ass belongs to me, now." I help her off my lap and onto her feet. Her legs wobble, and her eyes are glassy. "Now sit on that plug, open your knees and show me that pretty little pussy."

Summer blushes.

I tug her down to sit at the end of the couch, her back against the armrest. She gasps at the contact of the plug going deeper inside her.

"Hold your knees open."

Throwing me a doubtful look, she pulls her knees back to her shoulders, spreading her *pudenda* wide. Dew drips from her entrance, and her muscles shiver under my gaze.

Gathering some of her moisture, I bring the pad of my thumb to her clit and stroke ever-so-lightly in a circle around the sensitive nub. Her pelvic floor lifts, and one of her knees kicks out of her hand.

I arch a mock-stern brow. "Hold still for me, *principessa*."

She lets out a soft moan.

Again, I circle her clit with a feather-light touch.

"More, oh please, Carlo, more."

"Go stand in the corner." I point to a corner of my living room.

Her look of shocked disappointment is priceless. I lightly slap her inner thigh when she remains in position. Snapping her knees together, she struggles to stand and walks awkwardly, squeezing her ass together as if afraid the plug will fall out.

She looks hot as hell with my handprints on her ass and the handle of my plug marking the place I'll soon be taking her.

Standing at the juncture of the two walls, she slips her hand between her legs.

"Ah, ah. No touching. You don't get off until I say you get off. And right now, I want you in the corner thinking about who owns you."

She peeks over her shoulder, face flushed, eyes glassy and wild. *So fucking perfect.*

*   *   *

*Summer*

Oh, the torture. Every bit of me is on fire, burning for him. My ass tingles, my swollen clit throbs. The plug gives me a feeling of fullness, and my pussy, well, my pussy just feels empty. I'd give anything to have Carlo's cock in it right now. Or at least to have his powerful hands on me again, teasing, torturing, delivering pain and pleasure mixed into one.

But that doesn't seem to be part of his plan. I'm about to lose my anal virginity, which makes me nervous. But I need release. *Desperately.* How long will he make me wait? How much more torture can I take before I lose my mind?

"All right, *amore*, back over my lap."

I love the spanking. I could take any amount of pain, so long as I know it's for his pleasure. I was unsure for a moment last time because he'd been so relentless. I thought he might actually be mad. But no, this is sex for him. A game. Carlo is a sadist, and it turns him on to play this way.

If he's turned on, I'm turned on.

I trust him. When I was angry earlier, his only concern was to soothe me, to heal the rift between us. Now, though...now he's playing. Bringing us closer by demanding my vulnerability and trust.

I walk back to him, the plug in my ass making me acutely aware of each step.

"I changed my mind." His face is unreadable. "Get down on your hands and forearms and present that ass to me."

I drag my lower lip through my teeth as I obey, lowering myself to the position on his soft plush rug. I'm close enough to him that I smell his intoxicating scent, feel his body heat, his magnetic presence.

He lifts my ankles, splays my legs to straddle his waist, so I'm in a sexual version of the old wheelbarrow position.

"Carlo," I squeak in surprise. I'm totally bared to him, my ass and pussy open and centered over his lap, every private secret place accessible. The exposure, the humiliation, only makes my need flame hotter.

He grips the plug in my ass and pushes it in and out, fucking me with it.

I buck, squeezing my inner thighs together, finding his hard cock with my mons and rubbing my clit over it.

"Naughty girl," he murmurs, pulling the wicked plug out to stretch me wide, then shoving it in, over and over again.

"Carlo...Carlo, please." I need him, need him so badly.

He stuffs two fingers in my pussy, and I come, bucking and shivering.

The moment the orgasm stops, he starts spanking me again. It hurts a little more now, perhaps because of the orgasm, and yet I'd let him do anything to me. As the pain and heat grow louder, I begin to hump his clothed cock again, a second orgasm building from spanking alone.

Tears leak from my eyes—not of pain, simply from need for release. I need more, want more. Carlo can't hurt me enough. Each slap brings me closer and closer to ecstasy, jostling the plug in my ass until I thrash my legs, squeezing his waist and rubbing shamelessly.

Before I come a second time, he stops. Pulling out the plug, he rubs my hot cheeks, squeezes and grips my ass with a possessive, punitive grasp.

"Oh please..."

"Get up." His voice is rough. "Your gorgeous ass needs fucking."

I orgasm just from his words— a ripple of clenching in my core. Without his strong arm around my waist, helping me up, I wouldn't find my way back to vertical. I barely see the living room as he guides me to the bedroom.

"On your hands and knees on the bed."

I move without hesitation. Probably if he told me to throw myself off a rooftop at that point, I'd jump without even looking first.

I hear him rustling in a drawer, and then his hand grips my ankle. He fastens some kind of leather cuff around it.

"Spread your knees wider." I do so, and he slaps my inner thigh. The other ankle receives a similar cuff. "Crawl to the center of the bed."

When I move to obey, I realize he attached a bar between the two ankles, keeping my knees spread wide. The idea sends a fresh surge of lust rocketing through me.

"Face down on the bed."

I lower myself to my forearms and rest my forehead on the bed.

"Give me your wrists."

Oh God. This is beyond vulnerable. It's depraved. And of course, as frightening as I find it, I tremble with excitement. I turn my face to the side and reach back with my arms, bringing my wrists to my ankles.

He cuffs them both, attaching them to the same bar. My ass cheeks are spread wide for him now. His finger slides over my clit again, with more pressure this time—enough to pull a throaty cry from me.

Lube lands on my already stretched anus, and then Carlo's behind me, on his knees. He continues to tease my clit with an expert touch as he strokes his cock with more lubricant.

Thank God.

My pussy quivers and clenches. I pant in anticipation. Will it hurt? Will he stop if I don't like it?

Of course, he would. I trust him. Completely.

Carlo pushes the head of his cock against my entrance. "Deep breath in."

I suck in air in a shaky gulp.

"Blow it out, slowly."

As I exhale, he presses forward, prying me open with his huge cock.

I stop breathing and tighten against the intrusion, which of course, makes my anus burn.

"Take me."

Two words. A simple command, and yet it makes my thoughts spin out of my mind. My anus relaxes, and he presses forward, stretching me, filling me.

"Jesus, you're tight." His voice is low and gravelly. "So fucking tight." His hand wraps in my hair and pulls up while the fingers of his other hand still rub my clit. I couldn't be more owned by Carlo Romano than I am right now. And yes, I love it.

He eases back and pushes in, bumping my ass with his pelvis and pushing my face into the covers. He fills and empties me over and over again. It's far too much stimulation and yet somehow still not enough.

A high-pitched keening reaches my ears, but I wasn't aware of making any sounds, my sensations awash in color and light. His thrusts come faster, and my squeals grow louder.

He abandons my clit and pinches one nipple. The other hand threads under my waist and slaps my pussy, spanking my wet folds until I scream my orgasm. Carlo mutters a curse in Italian and shoves deep inside me, the heat of his cum filling me.

Somehow, he must've unbuckled my wrists because he guides me down to my belly. He shoves his cock even deeper, using his weight to sink into me, his fingers stroking my slit now.

He bites my neck, my ear, sucks at my neck, his breath hot with passion. He murmurs something in Italian that sounds like an endearment.

If I could move or speak, I'd ask him what he said, but I'm incapable of anything at the moment.

"You okay, *bambina*?" He eases out and rolls me to face him.

"Yes," I whisper, reaching for him because, already, he's too far away.

# Chapter Fourteen

*ummer*

S I scroll through my email on my phone as I sit on a bench between classes. The sun's out, and the NYU campus glimmers in burnished reds, amber and gold. Fallen leaves decorate the sidewalks and tree wells, their smell evoking fall.

An email pops into my inbox—from Ana Teasedale, my old dance teacher. I wrote her a long email, apologizing for leaving so abruptly and thanking her for the excellent technical base she gave me. I filled her in on the details of my career since I left, ending with my depressing choice to transfer to business school.

I nibble on my lower lip and open the email.

*Summer,*

*It's nice to hear from you. Why don't you come and guest teach for the Contemporary III class this week?*

That's it. Short and to the point.

So is this an audition for teaching more? Or just a one-time deal? The flutters of excitement surprise me. The contemporary III class is her advanced high school class. Teaching teens would be fun. I'd have no trouble giving the girls a class they'd love. Hopefully they'd beg Ana to have me back, and I'd have a job. Not that teaching one or two classes a week would pay my bills, but at least I'd be back to dancing—doing what I loved. Choreographing, even, which I've always wanted to do but was too intimidated to try in a professional setting. At my home dance studio, though, it would be easy. They'd need recital pieces, and I wouldn't need to worry about my professors or colleagues showing up and criticizing.

The more I think about it, the more I really hope this gig will work out. Even if I stay in business school and slowly kill my soul. At least I'd have this one creative outlet.

My phone rings, and Maggie's picture appears on the screen.

"Hey girl."

"Hey, what's up?"

"Nothing, just sitting on campus, killing time between classes. How about you?"

"Well, it's Pete's birthday this weekend, so I'm throwing him a party. Saturday at eight at our place."

"Oh." Pete's friends with John, which means he'll be there. In the close confines of their apartment.

"Come on, Summer. Don't be a chicken."

Of course, Maggie knows why I'm hesitating.

"Why don't you bring Carlo?"

Something in my solar plexus tightens. Bring Carlo? To Maggie and Pete's? That's like throwing a boxer on stage with ballerinas. Just...too different. Carlo looks mafia. He has danger written all over him. He dresses in fine Italian suits, and he carries a gun most of the time, as far as I can tell.

Anyone who hasn't guessed my family is Family with a capital "F" would get it when they saw me with him.

"I don't know, Maggie...I'm not sure how he'd mix."

"Oh, come on, what's the big deal? He's totally hot, and he has great manners. He'd get along fine."

I'm not sure if I can handle my worlds colliding that way. The two separate sides of me crashing together. Then again, maybe me showing up with a hot, attentive man would show John what he gave up. I would love for him to realize what a mistake he made.

As if Maggie could follow my thoughts, she says, "It would burn John up to see you with a new sexy man. Make him sorry he lost you."

"I know. It's tempting. But John knows Carlo. They've met at the few family dinners I brought him to. What if he thinks I'm dragging a cousin in and pretending to date him? That's a humiliating thought."

Maggie snorts. "You'll just have to make sure you're very un-cousinly with him. Somehow, I doubt that will be a problem."

I smile, remembering the crazy sex we had last night. Nope. Not a problem at all.

"Summer...I miss you. The whole gang misses you. Pete really wants you to come to the party. He asked specifically. He always asks how you're doing. Everyone does."

I sigh. "Okay, I'll ask Carlo." As soon as I said it, a wave of anxiety rushes over me. I don't know if I can stand to see John again.

"Awesome. I'm so glad. I can't wait to see you."

"Well, I didn't say I'd be there for sure."

"Please, Summer?"

"You're not taking no for an answer, are you?"

"Nope."

"Okay, I'll figure it out. I'll be there. Just don't be mad if I don't stay too long."

"I won't. Don't worry, it will be fine. You need to get over John. Pretend it never happened. He can't hurt you unless you let him."

I roll my eyes. "Thanks, counselor."

"It wouldn't hurt you to see one, you know."

"Ugh, enough, already. I'll be there. See you Saturday." I hit the end button before Maggie can annoy me further.

Eek. This party has disaster written all over it.

*Mario*

Every year a dozen lavender roses arrives for my mother without a card. She always cries and makes a big deal about it, going on about how my father must have arranged it before he died, but we both know that isn't true. Carlo sends the flowers.

No one ever speaks about what happened to my youngest brother. Word got around, probably even back to my mother about the circumstances around his disappearance. For the past four years, we've pretended like the guy never existed. My mother would stop herself from saying his name or turn her back abruptly to hide her tears when something reminds her.

My brothers, my cousins, they all keep their mouths shut. Ferdi looked over his shoulder, jumpy-like for a few years after Carlo left, but I know if Carlo wanted him dead, he would've done it while he had the chance. My little brother can be both decisive and ruthless.

That doesn't mean he won't show up to exact revenge on me someday. Frankly, I'm surprised it hasn't happened yet. I thought for sure it would've by now. Or at least that I would've heard something—that Carlo joined a rival organization or married a famous model. The guy isn't a coward, so he can't still be hiding. He must've found success somewhere else.

I tried to trace the flowers the first couple years, but each year the credit card holder had a different name and location. Dummy accounts. Carlo isn't stupid. That has never been his problem.

But perhaps I just haven't dug deep enough. It's time to get to the bottom of this. I can't have this Carlo-situation hanging over my head for the rest of my life. Picking up the delivery notice from the florist, I head out to pay them a visit. Someone has to know something. And I certainly have ways of making people talk.

*Summer*

I put on a micro-skirt and fitted sweater with a draped neckline. It hugs my breasts and shows off my cleavage while still looking relatively classy. I don a pair of brown leather high heel boots and survey myself in the mirror. *Eat your heart out John Jackson.*

When I come out to the living room where Carlo waits, he raises one eyebrow.

I cock a hip, my high-heeled boot jutting out to the side. "What?"

He purses his lips. "Please tell me you won't ever go out dressed like that without me."

His dominant act annoys me at the moment. "What's the big deal?"

He shakes his head. "Don't play games with me. You look like you're going out trolling. In this case, people will assume it's to please me, and I hope to God it is." He looks doubtful.

Heat creeps up my neck. Damn his ability to see through me. "Of course, it is," I say breezily, walking past him to the door. "Are you ready?"

He frowns but says nothing, reaching past me to hold the door open, as he always does. The perfect gentleman. The gentleman who holds doors open and ties women to the bedframe at night.

The party is already happening when we get there. I purposely timed it for us to arrive late, not wanting to suffer the early awkward part of the party when you have to actually talk to people. The music is up, as loud as they could play it without getting complaints from their neighbors.

"You're here!" Maggie's a little tipsy. She looks radiant in a red v-neck blouse and hip-hugging jeans.

"I'm here. We're here," I amend.

Carlo's hand rests at my low back. It feels possessive, like he's staking his claim on me.

"Hey Summer! Where have you been?" A friend, Jenny, rushes over and throws her arms around me. She smells of vodka. "It's great to see you." She peers up at Carlo with admiration.

"This is Carlo." I don't add "my boyfriend." It's not because I'm still worried that Carlo doesn't consider us a couple. He called me his girl, after all. It's more...well, I don't want to think about it now.

I glance around the apartment, trying not to flinch when I catch sight of John in the living room, sitting on the couch with his arm around a girl. My pulse races, and those feelings of unworthiness rush back.

Like I have something to prove to him, but he's already judged and condemned me.

Why did I even come?

Lifting my sternum, I adjust my blouse, glancing down to remind myself how hot my cleavage looks.

"What would you like to drink?" Carlo murmurs.

"Red wine, please. I'm just going to say hi to some

friends." I nod toward the living room. "I'll meet you in there." I rub my lips together and waltz in, a bright smile on my face. Inserting myself in the middle of the scene, I greet my old group of friends.

"Heeeey, it's Summer." Pete picks me up and squeezes me. He's definitely already drunk.

Oh, fuck.

It's all well and good to make John jealous, but Carlo is another story. Carlo is possessive as hell. All alpha male. Dangerous when provoked.

I steal a glance at him and see him sending a death glare in Pete's direction. He doesn't know this is Maggie's boyfriend. That it's harmless. He doesn't know this crowd at all.

I wriggle out of Pete's drunken hold. "Happy birthday, champ." I give him a friendly thump on the shoulder and step back.

I'm included in several simultaneous conversations, and I completely forget about Carlo until he shoulders his way through and hands me a plastic cup of wine.

I slip my hand into his. "Thank you." I beam up at him. This is how a boyfriend should be. Attentive. Protective.

Possessive.

I love feeling like I'm the center of Carlo's universe. So different from John, who thinks the world revolves around him.

I glance over at where John's sitting on the couch.

He's glancing my way.

Good.

I reach up and pull Carlo's face to mine for a showy kiss. If I were smart, I would pay attention to the way his brows come down when we pull apart, but instead, I'm looking back over to see John's reaction.

It's a good one. He looks like he wants to kick something, for sure.

Ha. Serves him right. Carlo is a real man. He was a child.

"Summer!" a friend calls from across the room, and I cross the room, Carlo in tow.

I make the rounds for a while. When John comes into the room, I wrap my arms around Carlo's middle and mold my body against his. He holds the back of my neck possessively. Intimately.

I love the way John abruptly turns and walks back out of the room.

Carlo unwinds his arms from me and leans in to say, "Hey, I'm going to go."

"What?" I blink. He wouldn't leave without me, would he?

"Why don't you stay at your place tonight since you're right here anyway?"

Only then does it occur to me that I messed up. "Oh." I look up in confusion, a little too tipsy to understand yet what happened. "You're leaving?"

"Yeah." He kisses me on the cheek. Not the lips. "I'll see you later."

"No, wait, I'll come."

"No." His expression is inscrutable, but I recognize the finality in it.

My skin prickles with warning. "Are you mad? Was it about Pete picking me up? Because he's Maggie's boyfriend. It was harmless."

"No, doll. I'm going to go. We'll talk tomorrow."

"No, Carlo—" I grab his arm. When I realize I've called attention to us, I release it.

He turns and walks away.

Grabbing my purse, I follow him out the door. "Carlo, hang on!"

He stops in the hallway, his face still unreadable.

"I'm coming with you." I catch up to him, but he doesn't move to escort me out.

He faces me and rubs his forehead. "*Bambina*, I can't do this."

"What?" My voice pitches up as the panic bleeds into my soul. What's he saying? My heart pounds in my ears.

"I don't think it's going to work out for us. The timing's bad. You weren't ready for a new relationship—you just needed a distraction and..." He sighs. "I don't want to be your sloppy seconds. It was arrogant of me to think I could make you forget about your douchebag ex, but clearly, I can't."

My vision blurs. "No, Carlo. I'm sorry. You're not sloppy seconds."

He doesn't look angry. His expression only holds regret. Or even sympathy. Well, yeah. He's the one breaking up with me.

"It's not your fault. You can't change what's in your heart. It is what it is. Go on, get back to the party—it's where you belong. I'll bring the kittens and your things over tomorrow."

I literally can't breathe.

And then he turns and walks off. Just like that.

Tears spill down my cheeks. "I don't belong there." My voice rises with a sob.

He doesn't turn around. Isn't going to rescue me from myself this time. It's over.

Turning, I rush back to Maggie's. I need a friend, and I don't care anymore what anyone at the party thinks of me. Including John.

Which is too bad because it's too late for that change of heart.

\* \* \*

*Carlo*

I drive home but don't go in. Instead, I sit in the parked SUV, staring into the darkness.

I'm fuck-all tired. Or maybe just numb.

I'm not pissed. It's my own fault for pursuing Summer. She wasn't ready. I made my move too soon.

I saw that window of opportunity, and I took it, but it was misplayed.

Tragically misplayed.

The heaviness that's descended on my chest has a familiar weight. The sense of betrayal isn't there like I had with Mario, but the loss is the same. The disappointment. The ache of loneliness that goes miles deep.

I lean my head back against the headrest and close

my eyes. I can't even face going into my apartment and seeing her things. Hearing the kittens scramble around all night exploring.

Sleeping in the car is better than facing the loss of Summer right now.

# Chapter 14

*C*arlo

I sit in the parking lot at Swank the next evening and look at the texts from Summer I've left unanswered. I haven't brought her things by yet —not because I'm not sure but because I can't see her yet. Especially not if she cries and tries to change my mind.

I'd do anything for her, but I'm not going to cage her into something when she isn't ready.

I want her love, and her heart is still tied up with the *coglione* John.

*Can we talk?*

*Carlo?*

*I'm so sorry about last night. I really want to tell you in person.*

I believe she's sorry. I'm sure she's upset thinking I'm mad. She's a pleaser, so it probably bothers her that I haven't answered.

I'm not trying to be a dick—I just haven't figured out

what to say. I'm too raw from it all. It's hard enough to accept she doesn't share my feelings. I'm sure as hell not ready to sit down and re-hash that fact with her.

It's my own fault. I shouldn't have moved so fast. I knew she wasn't ready to dive into a new relationship yet, but the moment I held her in my arms, I was unwilling to let her go. But it's time to smarten up. Maybe, in time, we can try again. Or maybe she'll never be interested in a guy like me.

My thumb hovers over the message. Fuck. The dominant in me—the guy who needs to take care of and protect her, even if she doesn't want me—can't leave her hanging. I care way too much about her.

*No apology necessary, Summer. If you need me, I'll be there, but as a friend.*

I send it and try to ignore the searing pain from my forehead.

She calls immediately. Fuck.

I'm not asshole enough to not take her call. I pick it up.

"Carlo. Thanks for answering. Can we just talk?"

I rub the place in my chest that aches. "Summer..."

"Please?"

"You're killing me, here."

"Will you just give me a chance to apologize? I screwed up. I behaved badly at the party and—"

"I can't do this, Summer," I interrupt. "I appreciate the apology, but it doesn't change the situation. The thing is"—I scrub my unshaven face with my hand—"my feelings for you are too real. Summer, I—"

I stop, shaking my head. Am I really going to tell her this?

Fuck it.

"This wasn't a new thing for me, *cara*. I've cared about you for years. I picked the wrong time to show you my feelings. You're not in a position to accept them now. It's okay. Maybe we can try again in the future."

"I'm ready to try again now," she pleads. "I'm over John, I swear—"

The squeezing in my chest worsens. I can't do this. "Let's give it some time. We both need some time."

"No, we don't."

"Summer." I put a little dominance in her name, and she sucks in a breath. "I'll see you at Sunday dinner."

"Yeah, okay." I hear tears in her voice, and I want to throw myself over a blade.

I never in a million years wanted to hurt her. Never thought I'd give her up once she pledged to be mine.

But the thing is, she isn't really mine. I don't want her heart borrowed from her *stronzo* ex. I don't want to be her back-up plan.

I want Summer, but I want all of her.

Heart, body and soul.

I sit in my car for a long moment then force myself to open the door and get out.

I go inside to lick my wounds over a few drinks.

Sonny's in the rear of the club where Joey recently installed a pool table for us, and we play a few rounds of pool. Normally I clean the table before the other guy ever takes a turn, but tonight, Sonny wins all three games.

"Something bothering you, boss?"

I shake my head, even though we both know my denial is a lie. Funny how three weeks with Summer changed everything for me. Despite the familiar surroundings and people, I feel as unmoored as I did that night Mario put a hit on me. I lost my home country, my family, my position that night.

I thought I found a new one here. The LaTorres fulfilled my need to belong, and I worked hard to secure my position.

Made myself indispensable to the don. Planned to marry his daughter to solidify things.

I craved Summer then, but it wasn't just the gorgeous young woman who was only seventeen–too young for me to even think of touching. It was what she represented. A secure place at the table. Permanency. A future.

Joey stepping back as next in line for the throne made my place even more secure. Made this imagined future even more attainable. And then Summer offering herself up to me on a platter?

Well, I just couldn't resist.

But now, I see that I jumped the gun. I did everything backwards. Leaping into a scorching sexual relationship with her before I ever took her on a date. Not getting the don's permission.

Not waiting until her broken heart over her ex had mended.

Now, as I toss back another Tanqueray and tonic, I've never felt so disconnected or alone. I'm not an American, not like them. I'm not actual family—at least not a blood relation—to any of them.

Summer complained she didn't know me, and I suppose it's true. No one here really understands me. Hell, do I even know myself?

"Want to play another game?" Sonny stands beside me, rubbing chalk on the tip of his pool cue.

"Nah."

"Oh shit…"

My gaze shoots up to follow Sonny's. Alexei's walking toward me with purpose. He looks high and furious as hell.

Sonny and I both palm our guns. Alexei would've been patted down for a gun by security at the door, but that doesn't mean he doesn't have one hidden somewhere. The moment he arrives, the Russian cocks his fist and lets it fly.

I block and deliver an uppercut to the gut. The Russian doubles over. Sonny presses the barrel of his gun behind the guy's ear.

"Walk to the back. Al doesn't like any scenes in here." We frog march the guy straight out the back door to the alleyway where Sonny and I let him go. "What the fuck?"

Alexei lunges for me again. Sonny follows, keeping his gun pressed to the guy's head. The Russian's pupils are tiny dots, his face unnaturally pale. The guy must've snorted five lines. He wraps his fist in my shirt. "Where is she?"

"Who, the girl?"

"Of course, the girl. Where is she? I need her back."

"You're not getting her back. She was mine, and I got rid of her. End of story."

"You gave her to the cops." He spits a little as he rasps in his thick Russian accent.

"Fuck you. Why would I give her to the cops, asshole? I used her, I sent her on her way. If the cops picked her up, that's not on me."

Alexei's eyes narrow to slits, and his breath hisses in and out of his nose. A bit of saliva gathers at the corner of his mouth. He says something in Russian that is obviously a string of insults.

I punch him in the stomach again. Sonny smacks the handle of his gun against the Russian's head.

"Get the fuck out of here. If I see your face here or at my game again, you're a dead man." I punch him one more time.

The guy crumples a little, but the drugs keep him from feeling much. We leave him in the alleyway and lock the door, letting Leo, the security guard know to never let him in again.

"He's gonna be trouble," Sonny warns as we walk toward Joey's office. "We shoulda capped him."

My nape prickles. Sonny's probably right. We haven't seen the last of the Russian.

We walk to the office in the back and tap on the door.

"Come in."

Cigar smoke fills the room, and Don Al sits in Joey's leather captain's chair, puffing on a cigar. Pauly, Bobby and Vince all lounge around, shooting the shit with him. Joey must be home with Sophie.

I plan on filling Al in on the situation with Alexei, but not when they're all lounging around like this.

"Hey guys." I accept the handshakes from the other men.

"Ah, here's the guy who's been keeping secrets." Vince's been drinking. He always had a bone to pick with me, acting like I don't deserve the position I have. He seems to think he ought to be in my shoes. But he's not that bright and makes bad decisions. Consistently. So even though he's family, he hasn't risen in the organization.

"What secrets?" Al's gaze is sharp.

I shrug. The only thing on my mind is the crazy fucking Russian and forgetting about Summer.

"Why don't you tell him?"

My lip curls. I'm not in the mood for one of Vince's challenges tonight. Hell, I'd gladly flatten the bastard. "Tell him what?"

"That you're fucking his daughter."

Oh, hell no.

Rage turns my vision to red. Nobody disrespects Summer like that. My body springs into action before thought even registers my decision. Our bodies crash to the floor with a thud, my fist smashing into Vince's face. "You don't ever talk about her that way," I growl through clenched teeth. I deliver another punch to Vince's jaw twice before I catch a blow to the mouth that busts my lip.

"Get him off." Don Al's tone holds heat. Which I guess is better than frost.

Pauly and Bobby haul me up and hold my arms, lifting me to face the Don.

Al walks around from behind the desk, his face a mask of anger. "Is that true?"

I yank my arm out of Pauly's grasp and wipe blood from my chin with the back of his hand. "I'm not *fucking* her. We were..." What? What can I possibly say that will keep the don from shooting me?

Al grips my shirt in his fist and yanks me close, his fist cocked. "*You were what?*"

"I'm in love with her." I sound like a pansy in front of the guys, but nothing less than the truth is worth uttering to Al about Summer.

Al's fist flies, and I let it land without dodging or defending myself because he's the don. Pain explodes in my eye, and I see stars as I slam back into the wall.

"You don't take from me." Al's still up in my face. "You don't take from me without asking first."

I close my eyes, weariness overcoming me.

"Look at me." Al's still fisting my shirt.

I open my eyes, not lifting my head from the wall. "It's over. It's over, anyway." Not that it matters to Al. A betrayal is a betrayal, I suppose. Al's right. I should've asked first. I was a fucking idiot.

Al's eyes narrow. "What the fuck do you mean, it's over?"

"I mean, I made a play for her, and it failed. She doesn't want me. She's still hung up on her ex. End of story."

Al's fingers ease from his shirt, and he steps back. He shakes his head. "Get out of my sight."

My brain shuts off completely. Numbly, I walk to the door and exit, not looking back. Am I permanently dismissed, or does Al just need time to cool down? How ironic that I originally wanted Summer to solidify my position in the Family, but touching her is what cost me everything.

And more ironic? I don't even care.

It must be my bludgeoned heart because I can't even muster a reaction to it. I wouldn't care if Al sent the guys out to cap me in the parking lot.

I just really didn't give a shit anymore.

*Summer*

There are so many moments in my life I wish I could have do-over. The night I fell for John's bullshit charm. That jump into the orchestra pit that shattered my foot. None of those even come close to how much I want to re-do Pete's birthday party.

I barely eat, too sick with regret. My apartment has never felt so lonely—not even when I first moved in, after my breakup with John. I haven't heard from Carlo since he texted yesterday.

I pick up my phone and call my mom. She's my second best friend.

As soon as I hear her voice, I start sniffling.

"Baby, what's wrong?"

"I screwed up," I tell her.

"Uh oh. Tell me what happened."

I tell my mom about dating Carlo–skipping the part about stripping at The Candy Store and our kinky sex sessions. Then I explain what happened at the party.

"Oh, honey. Sounds like you hurt his feelings."

It's crazy to think about someone as stoic and strong as Carlo getting hurt, but I realize she's right. I must have. "I acted like a self-involved pain in the ass," I agree. "He probably feels like I used him to make John jealous."

"Did you?"

I suck in a sobbing breath. "I guess I did. Which is so stupid. I wish I could go back in time and fix it all. I would have never gone to the dumb party. Or if I had, I'd only worry about what Carlo thought and felt."

My mom hesitates. "He told your dad you're still hung up on John."

"He talked to Dad?"

"Well,"—I hear a wry note in my mom's voice—"they had it out. I don't think your dad was happy about him going behind his back on this."

I go cold. "Is Carlo okay?"

"I'm sure he'll live."

"Did Dad hurt him?" My voice rises in pitch.

"Don't ask me things I don't know, baby." I hear the familiar note of warning in my mother's voice. It's not for us to know what goes on in the organization. They keep the women out of it. Some kind of Old World chivalry to protect us. Or sexism, depending on how you look at it.

"Are you still hung up on John?"

"No!" I answer immediately. I remember how I hadn't been able to forgive him. How I was hanging onto that resentment.

I guess that means I *was* hung up. But not anymore. Not when I know what it cost me. And as soon as I detach my blame from him, I realize it was never about John at all.

"I mean, maybe I was. But not on John, the actual person, more on what he represented."

"What do you mean?"

That old sense of failure and inferiority rise up, but for some reason, now that I'm faced with losing Carlo over it, I can see that it's stupid.

I don't need John to want me to believe I'm enough.

I honestly don't even need Carlo for that although he's the one who helped me gain my confidence back.

"I thought he was the measurement of whether I was good enough or desirable enough. But, of course, that was bologna."

"It's because he gaslit you," my mom says. "I might let your dad hurt him after all."

I realize suddenly how truly insignificant John is. He means absolutely nothing to me. I would never want to be with him again, and not from that place of anger and resentment that I held before. I mean, even if I'd never found out he cheated on me and we hadn't broken up, even if I still believed he was a decent guy—he's absolutely nothing compared to Carlo.

He brings nothing to the table. Has nothing to offer

me. I know now he was a judgmental, negative self-absorbed piece of crap.

And I don't care about any of it. I'm not bitter. I don't want to get even. I don't want him to know what he missed out on.

He's nothing to me.

He's nothing like Carlo. He never made me feel sexy or took charge of my body. He never gave me mind-blowing orgasms. He never cared about the details in my life or how I handled them. He belittled me. Talked down to me.

So different from Carlo's dominance.

Carlo...Carlo was amazing. He cooked for me, cared for me, protected and punished me.

And what did I do for him?

Zilch.

I didn't thank him. I was needy and insecure. I used him at the party, which must've been hard to take. Especially for an alpha man like him. And yet, he wasn't even angry. He just seemed sorry about the whole thing.

Which...hell. That means he truly cares. Can I make him care again? Make him give me another chance?

"Do you think I can fix things with Carlo?" I ask, my voice wavering.

My mom hesitates. "Do I think Carlo will give you another chance? Yes."

I hear my dad growl something in the background. It sounds threatening.

"Is that Dad? Tell him to leave Carlo alone."

"Carlo can handle himself with your dad. You go figure out how to make things right with him."

I suck in a breath. "Okay. I will. Thanks, Mom."

Pulling on my big-girl panties, I bake a batch of double chocolate brownies with nuts—the way he likes them—and arrange them on a plate, covering them with plastic wrap. It's not much, as far as gestures go, but it's the first thing I think of. Something I can do immediately. With love.

I need to see my sweet kittens and pick up my things, anyway.

Grabbing my purse, I take the brownies and head to my car. If Carlo won't take my calls, I'll just have to camp out at his apartment until he talks to me.

When I arrive, I don't see his car on the street. Ignoring the pounding of my heart, I take the elevator up to his place and knock on the door.

He doesn't answer, so I use my key to go in. The lock feels jammed, but then the door swings open.

Cookies and Cream run to me, mewing. Their little tails are lifted. They try to climb my legs. I set the brownies down and scoop them both up for a cuddle.

"Hi, my babies. I missed you so much, you sweet, furry things. How's my—"

I break off, realizing that something is terribly amiss in Carlo's apartment. The place is trashed. Drawers pulled out with their contents scattered all over the floor. Paintings off the walls are smashed on the floor.

My heart pounds.

Jesus. Did Carlo do this? Maybe he was angrier with me than I suspected. Or more torn up.

Then I hear a sound in the bedroom.

"Carlo?" My blood rushes in my ears. Is he okay?

Drunk or hungover, maybe?

I hesitate, then cautiously approach the bedroom, not sure what I'll find. "It's me. I just wanted to tal–"

Someone standing behind the door slaps a rough hand over my mouth as I step through, and a cold blade presses against my throat.

I scream against the sweaty palm that smells metallic and rank.

"Shut up," a thick Russian accent rasps in my ear.

I go cold. Understanding dawns.

I know who this is. The guy Carlo mentioned. The human trafficker.

I scream again. The knife blade punctures my skin. "I said shut up, or I'll cut up that pretty face of yours."

I frantically drag breath in through my nostrils and try to shut off the noise.

"I have gun in my pocket, but knives are better for women." He's breathing unnaturally hard, too. Like something's wrong with him.

"Should I carve up your face? Teach your *dago* boyfriend a lesson? Stain his floors with your blood? Hmm?"

I whimper, my gaze traveling frantically around the room, looking for anything that will help me escape.

"Get down. On your belly." He forces me down to

the ground and puts his knee in my back and pulls my wrists together.

I peer over my shoulder to see a greasy-haired man. Thin and sweaty. There's definitely something wrong with him. I've been sheltered my whole life, but I've seen this look sometimes on people on the street.

He's on drugs.

"Because of your boyfriend, police put a fucking tail on me. I had to move my operation." He duct tapes my wrists together.

"What do you want? Money?"

"No. It's very simple: Carlo lost my girl; I will take his."

"I'm not his girl." The fact that it's not a lie almost hurts worse than having my arms wrenched like this. My face pressed into the rug.

"Right. You are mine now. This is perfect." He seems to be muttering more to himself than to me now. "Viktor will get over his temper tantrum over me losing Mila. Perfect solution."

I realize I can't leave with this guy. If I do, I'll probably never come home. Risking him following through on his threat to cut my face, I let out the loudest scream I can muster.

And then my head smacks violently against the floor, and I black out.

I don't think I'm out for long because I'm still in the same position when my vision clears, only there's blood pouring from my nose.

"Get up. I have no intention of carrying you to the car." He hauls me roughly to my feet. "Let's go."

I lurch forward when he shoves me, tottering, my wrenched arms throwing off my balance.

He tosses his jacket over my shoulders–probably to hide the taped wrists. The knife blade prods my throat again. "You make one sound—one single sound—and I'll cut your tongue out. You understand, yes?"

Tears leak from my eyes, and I bob my head.

He yanks off the tape and drags me out of the apartment and down to the street.

I search frantically for someone to call out to, someone close enough to help, but there's no one.

My captor pops the trunk and shoves me inside then slams the door.

I scream and scream, but it doesn't matter. The car starts up and pulls away. I'm about to become this man's new sex slave.

# Chapter 15

*C*arlo

I'm driving from the docks to the poker game when my phone rings.

I haven't heard from Don Al since the night at Swank, but I go on as if I still belong in the organization. Until I hear differently, I still have responsibilities. A high-stakes game to run, managing the grappa shipment from my great uncle we smuggle in to avoid import tax. A new shipment of cell phones to be distributed to avoid taps or tracking.

I haven't decided what to do about Vince. Probably nothing, since he had the don's best interest in mind. I was in the wrong. He was right to call me on it.

I answer the call. "Uncle Junior." He's my one tie to my old life. I cling to my contact with Junior like a lifeline.

"Carlo. Mario paid me a visit."

"*Fanculo.*"

"He seemed to think I've been sending your mom flowers on her birthday."

I curse again.

"Of course, I didn't tell him anything. He's family too, but what he did wasn't right. We had a stare-down over *ammazzacaffè,* and when he stopped questioning me over the flowers, he asked about my exports."

*Fanculo, fanculo, fanculo.*

Mario's made the connection. If he hasn't already figured it out, he will soon.

"Well, if he comes, he comes. I'll be ready for him."

"That's why I'm warning you."

"Thanks, Junior. Everything on track for the next shipment?"

"Still on track. I'll tell you when it's in motion."

"Thanks, Junior. Talk to you later." I hit the end button and curse again.

My phone buzzes with a text, and I check it.

*No one fucks with Alexei.*

Oh, for fuck's sake. Clearly the Russian has been stewing. I let him live. My mistake. I need to talk to Al about taking care of this *stronzo.*

Of course, Al and I aren't exactly on the best of terms right now.

I consider a few threatening responses but decide not to reply at all.

Of course, that brings in another text. *You took my girl so I'm taking yours.*

I slam on the brakes and swerve to the side of the road, my heart pounding. This can't be... this has to be a bluff. How would he even know about Summer? Or where to find her?

I call Summer, wanting to rip the steering wheel off the car when she doesn't answer.

Tracking.

Her dad has a location tracker on her phone, and I gave myself access to it. I open the app, hoping to God I'll see her somewhere safe. At school. At her apartment. Anything.

But what I see turns my blood cold. She's at my apartment.

Which means, Alexei might actually have her.

I hit call. "Where is she?" I snarl when Alexei answers.

Alexei laughs. "You got my message."

"*Where. Is. She?*" I bellow.

He chuckles again. "You think we're bargaining. We're not. I'm not holding your girl hostage. I'm keeping her. I want you to remember. *No one fucks with Alexei.*"

"She's not mine. You took *the don's fucking daughter.* If you touch one hair on her—"

Alexei ends the call.

Fuck. I slam my fist into the dashboard over and over again.

Summer.

I have to get her back before that maniac does anything to her.

I have to rescue my girl, but I don't even know where to start.

I force myself to push the red haze of rage out of my mind and drag oxygen in through my nostrils.

And then it comes to me.

There is one man who might be able to help.

I call Sonny, first. "Game is canceled," I bark. "I need you and Vince on standby for a war. Gather weapons, be ready to move."

"What is it, boss?"

"The *cazzo* Russian took Summer."

"What? Fuck."

I end the call and dial Detective Bailey.

"Carlo."

"Alexei picked up my girl--the don's daughter. I need help. A location. Anything you have."

Detective Bailey blows out his breath.

"Please." I'm not above begging. I did this guy a favor. He owes me one back.

"Yeah, we lost the tail on him earlier, but there's a location he frequents–where he buys his drugs. I'm staking it out now. I'll text you the address."

I screech into the road to find the drug dealer and make him talk. Every second feels critical. Every fucking second the Russian has Summer means...I couldn't even go there.

My phone rings with a call from Bailey.

"He just dropped by and is moving again. I'm on his tail." He gives me the street and direction he's headed, and I make a screaming left turn across traffic to change my trajectory.

"Was she with him? Summer? *Was there a girl with him?*"

"Negative. He's alone."

My heart pumps. Was he bluffing?

Either way, he's a dead man. I still have to chase him down and kill the motherfucker.

"He stopped. I'll drop you a pin."

Thank fuck.

"Bailey. When I get there, Alexei's mine."

There's a moment of silence, and then the detective says, "It may take me a while to get parked for my stake-out."

"He won't walk away from this."

"I didn't hear that." Bailey ends the call.

I texted every soldier in the organization. *Russians took Summer LaTorre. All guns needed at 5458 Palmer Drive.*

I hit send and call Al before the don calls me. "What the fuck?" Al yells.

"I don't know. Her phone is at my apartment. He must've found her there. He's a junkie." That's the only explanation I can come up with for the shit-brain's actions. "I'm going to kill every last one of them."

"Not if I get there first." Al ends the call.

I scream through the streets, running red lights and screeching the tires around curves. I only slow when I approach the house to avoid alerting the occupants.

The address is in a seedy part of town, not far from

where he got his drugs. I grab my spare gun from the glove box and get out, a pistol in each hand. A half block down and across the street, I see a man sitting behind the wheel of a dark sedan.

I aim my Ruger, squinting in the darkness.

The interior light of the car came on, illuminating the face of Michael Bailey, the detective.

I lower the gun. Okay, then. He's letting me have this. I don't care if he comes in and arrests me when it's over.

All I care about is saving Summer.

I should wait for backup, but I can't. Every second Summer's in danger takes ten years from my life. I go in alone, shooting the lock off the door and slamming my shoulder into the wood to break it open.

Someone fires on me, and I pull back, but not before I aim and fire at the guy pulling the trigger. He goes down.

I go inside as three men storm up a flight of stairs that must lead from a basement. I jump back when one of them fires. Wood from the doorframe splinters in my face. I shove my Ruger around the corner and risk a quick look to aim. I pull the trigger as more shots rain from them.

From the sound of it, one body hits the ground. I shoot and another falls. The third guy fires until his gun runs out of ammo, and I step out, shooting him between the eyes.

I jog past their gasping bodies.

In the basement, I find a dozen or more girls, scantily dressed and looking high. Alexei stumbles forward, fumbling for the gun in his holster.

*Where in the hell is Summer?*

I shoot each of Alexei's kneecaps. The man screams, falling to the floor and writhing. I take his gun and two knives, then kick his ribs, hard. "Where is she?"

"Carlo?" I hear Sonny upstairs.

"Down here. Search up there for Summer."

Alexei groans and mumbles something.

I kick him again. "Where is she?" I snarl between clenched teeth.

The bastard chuckles.

I drop to my knees beside him. Search his pockets. I find a bag of cocaine. I pull out his phone, but the last call made was to my phone. Nothing pertinent in the texts.

I grasp his shirt in my fist, pick up his head and slam it back into the floor. "Who has her? *Where's. My. Girl?*"

Alexei's unfocused gaze swings around the room, scanning the girls huddled on cots. He appears genuinely confused.

"What girl?" one of the young women says in a thick Russian accent.

"*My* girl," I roar. "The one he came in with."

"He didn't bring a girl."

Cold fear pierces my heart. "What?" I surge to my feet.

She shrinks, and I have to stop myself from advancing on her and scaring her further. "He came alone--no girl." She shakes her head emphatically.

*Fanculo.*

"How long ago did he arrive?"

She looks at me blankly.

*"When?"* I tap my Rolex. "When did he get here?"

"Thirty minutes, no more."

Thirty minutes. Was that time for him to have sold her to someone? His drug dealer, maybe, since he obviously has a fresh supply. But Bailey had said he was alone.

I run up the steps, two at a time.

"No sign of her upstairs, boss," Sonny calls down.

"Go sit on the Russian, see if you can make him talk." I stalk outside.

Outside, the detective still sits in his car, watching. Al's pulling up. Oh God, how will I tell him his daughter isn't safe yet? I want to kill the fucking Russian a million times over.

I push the rage down and try to think.

The trunk. The trunk of his car.

That's where he had the last girl during the game.

I scan the street for the car and see it. I jog toward it without saying anything to Al.

"Where is she?" he snarls, jogging after me.

As soon as I get to the car, I bellow, "Summer?"

*"Carlo!"* The muffled sound comes from the trunk.

For fuck's sake. The guy must've been so high he forgot about her in the trunk.

"Summer!" I yank on the handle to open the trunk, but it doesn't yield. "Hang on, *cara*. I'm going to get you out."

"Carlo, Carlo, *please*. Get me out of here."

Oh God, the fear in her voice makes me want to rip the car apart with my bare hands.

Al shoots the window to the driver's side out and reaches in to pop the trunk.

I throw it open. Summer lies inside, her hands duct-taped together. Blood covers her face. She blinks at the light, struggling to push herself up.

"Hang on, baby." My voice shakes as I cut through the tape.

She throws herself into my arms the moment I have her free. "I knew you'd come for me."

Her words cut me like glass. This was my fault. I'm not the hero here.

"Who did this? Is he still alive?" There's murder on Al's face.

My jaw flexes. "Not for long."

"Where? In there? I'll take care of it."

I nod. "I'm getting Summer out of here." I want to be the one to kill Alexei myself, but Summer's my priority.

Across the street, Detective Bailey climbs out of his car. I hear sirens in the distance. We're running out of time.

Al points his gun in the detective's direction as he walks swiftly toward the door of the house.

"Detective Bailey gave me the address here," I intercede.

Al drops his arm. "Detective," he calls out. "I'll just be a minute."

"*One* minute," Bailey warns.

"Appreciate it." Don Al stalks into the house, his pistol in his hand, his two soldiers flanking him.

I pass the detective on the way to my Mercedes SUV.

"The girls are in the basement. The rest of the house will be clear when we're through."

He nods.

"I owe you."

Detective Bailey shrugs. "Glad you got your girl back."

# Chapter 16

*Summer*

Carlo carries me to his SUV and eases me into the passenger side seat. He inspects me, his hands frantically moving over my body. "Are you okay, baby? Do I need to take you to a hospital?"

My head hurts from banging against the floor, but my nose stopped bleeding.

"No, no hospital."

"Did he–" Carlo breaks off, a black rage brewing behind his hazel eyes.

"No," I say quickly, to alleviate his fear.

"Thank fuck."

"He was bringing me to his boss, Viktor."

I shiver, and Carlo shrugs out of his suit jacket and drapes it across me. "I'm going to get us out of here before the cops show, okay, *cara*? And then I'll take care of you."

He shuts the door and runs around to the driver's

side, jumping in and taking off before he's put on his seat belt.

I drink in the sight of him. His eye is black, and there's a bruise on his jaw, my beautiful warrior.

"I knew you'd come."

I see pain in his expression. He's probably blaming himself for this.

"Carlo–"

He reaches for my hand and pulls my fingers to his lips, kissing them. "It's okay, *bambina*. Everything's going to be okay."

"Is it?" I croak.

Because I'm less worried about what just happened to me than I am about what's going on between us. Our bruises will heal, but I need to mend our hearts. I need to make Carlo understand what he means to me. That he's so much more than I made him believe.

"You mean with us?"

"I'm sorry I screwed up, Carlo--"

"It's okay, *principessa*," he cuts in.

"No wait–just let me finish. I love you, Carlo. I was at your place to try to make you believe it."

He stills, eyes on the road. I see his Adam's apple bob.

"I've worshipped you since the day you showed up at our house. What I feel for you doesn't even come close to...no, I don't even want to compare. John wasn't even real. He was...nothing but an outward reflection of how I felt about myself. I was trying to prove something. That I fit in. That I was desirable. And the only reason I thought I cared about him was because I somehow thought if he liked me, it meant I was doing something right. But none of that was love."

Carlo still won't look over. His breath sounds ragged. His hands grip and regrip the steering wheel.

Tears of regret fill my eyes. "I'm sorry it took me too long to figure that all out. I didn't mean to hurt you."

Now he finally looks at me. "*Principessa.*" He sounds choked. He reaches out and brushes my hair back from my face with more tenderness than I've ever received. "I would take a million blows if it meant having you at the end of it all."

I let out a sob-laugh. "There won't be anymore."

Carlo's lips twist wryly. "I'm not sure about that. Your dad's going to kill me for this." His jaw flexes. "I'm so sorry you got hurt because of me."

"I would take a million blows if it meant having you at the end of it all," I whisper his words back to him.

Carlo pulls up in front of his apartment and helps me out of the car then swings me up into his arms.

"My legs aren't hurt," I protest, nuzzling my face into his neck.

"I don't care. I'm carrying you." There's a stubborn note to his voice. Almost like he's not going to let me leave his arms again.

I try very hard not to swoon.

"Are we okay?"

"Yeah, baby, we're okay." His tone is soft and indulgent.

"Are we back together?"

The corners of his lips hike up. "You sure you want me?"

"I'm positive. You're all I want. The only man for me."

"Then you're mine." His lips find my neck, and he kisses and nibbles at it as he carries me up the stairs and into his apartment.

"*Fanculo,*" he curses softly when he sees the state of the place.

"I know."

"You came here to see me?"

"Yeah." I shudder remembering.

He lowers me slowly to my feet. Cookies and Cream come running and mewing, and I scoop them both up. "He...did this while you were here?"

"No. It was like this when I got here. He stood behind the bedroom door and grabbed me when I came through."

Carlo curses again, dragging a hand through his hair. "I should've been the one to kill him." I see the danger behind his glower and shiver again.

Carlo's gaze falls on the plate of brownies I brought over. His expression softens. The murder falls away. "You baked for me."

"I know it's dumb, I just wanted to do something–"

He catches my face in his hands. "Not dumb. Sweet. You're so sweet. Come here, *principessa.*" He urges me onto the couch. "Let's get some ice on your face."

He wraps an icepack in a towel, and I hold the ice to my nose and forehead.

"It looks like you need some, too." I eye the purple swelling around his eye and on his jaw.

"Me? No." He dismisses my concern.

"Take this." He returns and hands me three ibuprofen and a bottle of water, and I swallow them down. Carlo sits beside me and gathers me against his body, one arm wrapped protectively behind me. "Come here, *bambina*. I need to hold you."

I curl into him with the kittens purring in my lap and my legs tangled over his.

"*Bambina*...I'm so sorry this happened to you," he chokes.

"It wasn't your fault." I loop my arms around his neck. "And I'm fine."

Maybe it's a sign of what a spoiled mafia princess I really am, but I had every confidence that Carlo would show up to rescue me. I never doubted for a minute and that faith in him cushioned me from experiencing any emotional trauma. Honestly, I'm glad it happened, if it's what threw us back together.

Maybe I should be shaken up over the deaths of the Russians–I heard the gunshots and can only assume what happened–but I feel buffered from that somehow, too. Carlo and my father did what they had to do. I don't question it or judge it. I knew Carlo was a warrior, like my father. Not a man to stand back when confronted.

He strokes my face, looking beyond the bruises and truly studying me. His hazel eyes hold concern, but some of the anguish falls away as I look steadily back at him.

"I'm okay."

"You're brave."

I shake my head. "No. I just knew you'd come for me."

He blinks rapidly and leans his forehead against mine. "I won't let anything like this happen to you again. I promise."

"You can't control everything, Carlo. Bad things happen. Just don't leave me again."

One corner of his mouth kicks up then falls back into place as he sobers. "Never," he says fiercely. "Not even if your dad kills me for it."

As if conjured by his words, my dad throws open the door like he owns the place and casts a grim look at the mayhem before landing on us.

\* \* \*

\* \* \*

*Carlo*

"Are you okay, baby?" Al asks Summer.

She leans her head on my shoulder as if to prove we're one unit and nods. "I'm fine. Carlo gave me some ibuprofen."

Don Alberto arches a disbelieving brow.

Honestly, I'm surprised how smoothly Summer took all this, as well, but my girl seems far less traumatized by her kidnapping than she was by our breakup. She's stronger than any Made man. Stronger than steel because she's held together by love and kindness. Because she's flexible and she flows.

"I would prefer we didn't tell your mother about this," Al says, proving there's someone he has to bend for, as well.

"Yeah. Probably a good idea to keep it from her," Summer agrees.

Apparently satisfied, Al pins me with a glower.

He was pissed at me to begin with, and now I'm responsible for his daughter getting kidnapped. I'll be lucky if he doesn't march me out to the woods and make me dig my own grave.

He isn't holding a gun at the moment, though, so we're probably okay. I'd gladly take as many punches as he wants to throw and all his piss and vinegar in exchange for the right to hold his daughter.

Al takes in our position with narrowed eyes. "I see you two worked out your differences?"

When I nod, he tips his head toward the door to my balcony. "I need a word with you alone."

Summer stiffens. "Is it about me?"

"It's between me and Carlo." Al edges his voice with authority.

"If it's about me, then I'm going to be there." She swings her legs off my lap and thrusts her chin forward.

"Summer. It's okay, *bambina*." I drop a kiss on her forehead before I stand then follow Al out onto the balcony and shut the door.

Al folds his arms across his chest. "You're going to marry her."

"Damn straight I am." It's not like she's pregnant, and we aren't in the 1950's, but I get it. The underboss screwing the don's daughter is disrespectful, to say the least. Al needs to know my intentions are pure.

Al turns to look at my view, pulling out two cigars and trimming them. Handing one to me, he lights his and passes the lighter. I take it, my face composed into a blank mask.

Al chews on the end of his and contemplates me.

"I've trusted you. Thought I knew you. I know your weaknesses, which are also your strengths."

I wait to see where he's going with this.

"I see the way you look over your shoulder at the other men, never trusting anyone but me. Maybe Joey, now that he's not a threat. Even if my Zia Maria didn't tell me why you had to come to America, I would've known you carried baggage related to trusting those closest to you.

"But this thing with Summer" He shakes his head. "I missed it. But I suppose I was blind. Carmen said she's always known you had a thing for her."

I light my cigar and puff.

"That true?"

"That I've always had a thing for her? Si."

"Because she's my daughter or because of Summer?"

I know what he's asking me. Whether this is a political move or one of the heart.

"Because of Summer."

He nods, chomping on his cigar. Looking out at the street below. "Yeah, you would've done it right if your heart wasn't involved. You usually have a clear head with what's required in a situation."

Regret washes over me. Al's given me everything I have in this world right now. He's the last person I wanted to offend. "I'm sorry I fucked it up. I didn't mean to disrespect you. It happened sort of quickly, and then I couldn't take a step back."

Al says nothing for a long moment. I have no idea what's in the guy's head. He still may be contemplating my death or deportation for all I know.

"I wouldn't have picked you for her."

"I know."

Al waits, as if to see if I have anything to say for myself.

Picking up the cue, I spread my hands. "I told you before, I'm not fucking with Summer. I will honor her and treat her like a princess until the day I die. I won't cheat. I won't let her down. You can count on me to take care of her and give her everything I have."

Al finally swivels his head and pins me with a hard gaze. "You ever plan on moving back to Sicily?"

I don't hesitate. "You know I don't."

He nods like he's satisfied with that answer. He doesn't want me taking his baby away from his family.

"She loves you."

I shrug. "She might. She might just think she needs me. But *I* love *her*."

"No. I know my daughter. She wasn't even shaken up by getting knocked around, tied up and thrown in a trunk. She's in love."

I can't stop myself from glancing back to the door, to where the woman I adore is still sitting on my couch. Willing. Waiting for me. Mine, whether this man gives me permission to take her or not.

"I'm not ready for Summer to be married, but then, I wasn't ready for her to graduate high school either. Or go to college. Or have a boyfriend."

"I'll put a ring on her finger tomorrow, but we can wait as long as you want," I offer.

Al goes on as if he didn't hear me. "Carmen won't be crazy about Summer's life continuing to be entrenched in the family business, but she loves you as much as I do."

I look over, my breath stalling. Heart thudding.

"You're the son I don't have."

I don't move. I try to keep my face blank, but I can't breathe.

"I'd be proud to have that relationship formalized with marriage."

A muscle in my face jumps, and I angle my face away to cover the emotion. I extend my hand.

Al ignores my hand, embracing me and kissing me on both cheeks. He claps me on the cheek. "You take good care of her."

When we pull away, I have to blink rapidly.

"And I don't want her calling her mom crying over you again—"

"It won't happen."

"I don't care whose fault it was, I don't want to hear that."

"I know, I know." I shake my head. "That was my mistake. I didn't think she—"

He waves off the explanation. "I really don't want to get in the middle of it. Just make sure it doesn't happen again."

"*Lo giuro su Dio.*" I swear to God.

*Summer*

My dad leaves, and I press myself against Carlo, my breasts flattening against his ribs. He brushes a strand of hair from my face. "I'm going to marry you, *bambina*."

I stiffen. "Because my dad said you had to?"

"No. Because you belong to me."

I blink up at him, a smile growing. Carlo is mine. I'm his.

He tips his head toward the bedroom. "Now go in there. I need you naked and squirming beneath me."

A familiar zing of excitement shoots straight to my core. The words *you belong to me* fill all the empty places in my soul. All my confusion about who I am, or what my future ought to hold fall away. None of it matters so long as I belong to Carlo, because he has the ability to make everything perfect. To make it right. He knows me. He understands who I really am, perhaps better than I understand myself. So if I belong to a man like that, I have nothing to fear.

"Do I have time for a shower?"

Carlo surveys me with a heavy-lidded gaze. He's in

his dominant role. "Make it quick, *bambina*. I'm hungry for you."

I go to the en suite bathroom and turn the water on hot. When I strip and step under the spray, I groan. It feels so good, shedding the entire week of heartache under the spray of water. I don't stay in until the mirrors are fogged, though. Carlo said to make it quick. Turning off the water, I step out and towel off, then wrap the towel around my head to dry my thick hair.

Carlo saunters in. "On your knees."

I toss the towel back into the bathroom and drop to my knees, palms up on my thighs, waiting. My heart pitter-patters in fluttery anticipation.

He walks to me and shoves his fingers through my damp hair. "Good girl." He grasps the hair and pulls my head back. "Who do you belong to?"

"You, Carlo. I belong to you."

He rolls my nipple between his fingers and thumb. "Does this body belong to me?"

"Yes."

He brushes the backs of his fingers across my chest, stopping above my beating heart. "What about this heart?" he asks the question softly, losing the dominant pitch of his voice. Like he's not entirely sure of my answer.

I'm sure.

"Yours." I unzip his pants, and his cock springs out. My breasts ache as I reach for him. I grip the base and squeeze. Hard. "I'm only yours."

He strokes my hair. "Sweet girl." There's an ache of

happiness in his voice. A choked emotion, like he can't believe it's true.

I swirl my tongue around the underside of the head of his cock, flick the tip and blow on it to let it cool, then engulf him completely. He groans, his fist tightening in my hair. He lets me set the pace for a while, and then he begins thrusting, holding my head immobile and using me.

"That's it, *bambi*, you take my cock like such a good girl."

I orgasm a little just from his words. My pussy pulses in time with my heartbeat, my clit throbs with need. Empty, empty. My pussy feels so empty. I hollow out my cheeks and suck hard, even with his hectic thrusts.

"Enough. I need you underneath me." He grasps my upper arms and lifts me to his chest, holding me against him and kissing my damp head. He strokes down my naked back, cupping and kneading my ass.

He pushes me backward, onto the bed. Crawling over me, he pins my arms up by my head. I arch, lifting my lips and moaning wantonly.

"You want me to fuck you properly?" he asks.

"Yes, please," I moan.

"I'll pound into that greedy little pussy until you can't walk straight," he warns.

"Oh God." I struggle against his grasp on my wrist, thrust my pussy toward his cock. "Do it now, Carlo."

A smile glimmers. "After your clit torture." He releases my wrists and crawls down between my legs, wrapping his arms around my thighs to hold them open.

He licks and flicks, sucks and nibbles at my clit until I writhe in agony, desperate for release. I know it probably serves to give him time to get hard again after his climax, but it seems so cruel when I'm desperate for him.

"Penetration. I need you inside me. Oh please, Carlo, why won't you fuck me?"

He chuckles. "I will definitely fuck you, *bambina*. I can't wait to feel your hot little cunt squeezing my cock."

"*Now,* Carlo."

"Up on your knees and forearms," he commands. Grasping my hips, he buries his cock in one deep stroke, but there's no pain. I'm long past wet and ready. I'm the slip-and-slide at the waterpark, and he's pumping into me, the slick sounds of our contact accented with the smack of flesh against flesh.

He thrusts into me hard, ruthlessly. He bends my wrists behind my back and grips my elbows for leverage, giving me the feeling of a forced sex act.

My eyes roll back in my head. Even before my orgasm, I rocket to outer space, losing all rational thought, all coherency, flying higher and higher until he cracks me open, and I explode into pure sensation—ripples of release, even more gushing fluid, the endless squeezing of my muscles around his cock.

He gives a shout and finds his own finish, buried balls deep, pushing me down to my belly, where he covers me like a blanket.

"Mine," he murmurs.

"Yours."

He eases out of me eventually and gathers me up into

his arms. "Marry me, *principessa*." His stare is intent. Loaded. "We'll get you a ring tomorrow."

"Yes."

His face breaks into a smile.

"*Sì?*"

"*Sì*. Yes, I will marry you, Carlo Romano."

"Soon. I want to marry you soon. No long engagement and a year's worth of planning."

"Afraid I'll change my mind?"

He grins. "Maybe. A little. Or maybe I'm sick of waiting. It's been *four years*."

My eyes fill with tears, and once again, I wonder how I could have missed this miraculous affection he held for me.

He cups my face and strokes his thumb along my cheek with a tenderness, a reverence. "I love you, Summer LaTorre."

"And I love you."

# Chapter 17

*arlo*

C I stand in front of the hotel mirror and tie the bowtie on my tuxedo. I checked into the honeymoon suite before the wedding to bring up our suitcases and put the 1988 Moet and Chandon Dom Perignon on ice for later.

I pick up the boutonniere—a pale pink rose—and pin it on my lapel. Summer chose pink roses as her wedding flower because that's what I always bring her. Not wanting to disappoint, I had the suite filled with dozens of them and petals scattered on the bed, across the counter of the sink and in the tub.

I check my phone. It's early, but there's nothing left to do. I might as well head to the church where I can greet the early arrivals. I pick up my keys and head to the elevator. We were lucky enough to nab a reception hall at the Ritz Carlton, thanks to a last-minute cancellation. Normally the hotel is booked nine months out.

Carmen was disappointed about the short engagement, but Summer was perfectly serene in facing down her mother. Actually, she's perfectly serene in general. Any last misgivings I had about her not really loving me, only needing me, evaporated as I've watched a quiet happiness bloom in her.

Not even the stress of wedding planning bothered her—she approached it all with enthusiasm. Carmen wanted things big and fancy, and Summer had her own ideas, but they found ways to compromise.

Her career shifted, too. All on her own, she picked up several teaching gigs, working mostly with children, and she plans to finish business school and then to apply to a Master's program in Dance/Movement Therapy at Columbia.

In the car, I remove my gun and holster and stash it in the glove box. I've worn a gun in church before, but at my own wedding, it seems wrong. My bride shouldn't have to be reminded of the danger in my life on the day she commits to make a life with me.

*Mario*

It's cold in New Jersey in November. My two capos and I sit in the rental car with the heat on full blast outside Alberto LaTorre's house. There's been a lot of activity—vehicles coming and going. People carrying boxes out to cars. Carrying hair dryers and curling irons inside. Now a white limo sits out front. Must be a big occasion—a wedding, maybe.

I tracked my Uncle Junior's grappa exports to the LaTorre family in the Newark area. Forest Hill, to be precise. The don is some kind of relative of my Zia Maria —a nephew, maybe.

This might be a wild goose chase—I have no evidence that Carlo's in America—but I had to come check it out for myself.

The door swings open again, and I lift the binoculars, feeling more like a cop than the don of the most powerful crime family in Sicily. Several people exit, getting into the various cars parked within the gated property. Sure enough, a beautiful girl in a merengue of white tulle emerges, flanked by an older couple who must be her parents and three young women—two of them twins—in bridesmaid's dresses.

I put the car in drive and pull away, turning down a side street, where we won't be noticed. If Carlo's part of the LaTorre Family, he'll be at the wedding, and my men and I can probably blend in, unnoticed. There will be no better place to get a bead on my baby brother.

I idle until the limo passes and let two more cars follow before I pull out to stay on their tail. They weave through the suburb with its towering trees, the branches glittering with a coat of ice. Snow begins to fall—big wet flakes that melt on my windshield as soon as they land.

The limo pulls into a parking lot of a Catholic church bearing the name St. Mary's Cathedral. I accelerate and drive past, taking a trip back to the main street to get a coffee. Better to show up late to the wedding than be noticed as early arrivals.

An hour later, I drive back. Good thing we always dress sharp, so we look ready for a wedding.

We head in and sit on the bride's side in the very back, just as the wedding march music begins.

The bridesmaids file in—twins and another young woman, all about the same age as the bride.

Two little flower girls giggle and throw pink rose petals which catch in the froth of white skirts.

And then the groom. I stop breathing for a moment when I realize the groom is Carlo. So my baby brother is marrying into the LaTorre family. He always was smart and ambitious. He knew exactly how to secure his place.

Carlo looks older and yet unchanged—still the same proud face, our mother's hazel eyes looking out with cool appraisal, even on his wedding day.

I shift behind Tony, who Carlo doesn't know, to block the view of my face.

Carlo walks to the altar, drops to his knee and makes the sign of the cross. When he straightens, he has eyes only for his bride, who's walking down the aisle on Alberto LaTorre's arm.

I assume the marriage is political in nature, not that I doubted my brother would play the part of doting husband to a "tee", but Carlo's stoic mask crumbles as he watches the beautiful young woman walk toward him. His eyes redden, his nostrils flare. The two stare at each other, and she, too, grows teary, then giggles a little and leans on her father.

I didn't doubt Carlo would find success wherever he landed, but seeing him in love makes my chest tighten. His life hasn't been a complete misery, then.

An older woman sings Ave Maria, and the ceremony proceeds in Latin. Carlo's focus remains on the priest or his bride until he kisses her like she's the most precious treasure he could hold, and they turn to their guests. Only then does his gaze land on me and his body goes perfectly still.

His new wife smiles tearfully as he walks her down the aisle, but Carlo's face is made of stone.

My aisle is the first to exit, and we're handed little plastic bottles of bubbles with the instructions to wait outside the church and blow. I toss mine in a frozen flower bed and walk to our rental car and lean against it. I have no doubt Carlo will find me here.

* * *

*Carlo*

"Give me your gun." I grab Sonny's arm and yank him back into a church hallway.

"What is it?"

"My brother is here from Sicily."

Sonny looks at me blankly.

"My brother Mario. I left Italy because he wants me dead. Give me your fucking gun." I yank it out of the guy's holster and shove it in my jacket pocket.

"There you are. We're supposed to be doing photos." Al sticks his head around the corner. He must notice our deadly expressions because his battle face appears. "What's going on?"

"Mario's here. My brother."

Al's hand goes to his gun. "I'll take care of it. You go take care of my daughter."

I grit my teeth. "No. I have to take care of this myself." I push past my father-in-law and find an exit to the church, my fingers closed around the handle of the gun, safety off.

Al and Sonny are right behind me.

"Hey what's—" Joey catches them in the hallway and joins the parade.

I pause and put my hand on Sonny's chest, stopping him. "You're not armed. You stay in here. Joey, do you—"

Joey pulls back his jacket to show me he's strapped.

"No, Joey's not involved in this shit. Give your gun to Sonny," Al orders.

"What the fuck is going on?" Joey demands.

"Carlo's brother showed up."

Joey purses his lips and reluctantly turns his gun over to Sonny. "I'll stall the women. Make this come out right —it's a fucking wedding."

"Like we need advice from you," Al mutters as we file out the door and into the parking lot.

Mario stands by a car, flanked by his two men, clearly waiting for me.

Someone ought to pray for my soul because I aim my gun at my brother's forehead, right there outside St. Mary's Cathedral. I walk swiftly forward, my gun arm steady.

Mario doesn't move. His men stiffen, looking warily at the three armed men approaching. None of them reach for their guns. I press the muzzle of my Ruger against his skull.

"I'm not here to kill you," Mario says easily. "If you want to commit murder on your wedding day, that's on you."

I suck in my breath, the searing pain of my brother's betrayal still as fresh as the day he tried to have me killed. Suddenly I'm that young man again—shocked to the core, unable to believe my own brother wanted me dead. Slowly grasping the enormity of my loss because even though I lived, my life was stripped from me.

Mario holds his palms up, without making any quick movements. "I came to make amends. I was wrong. I sinned against you, and our mother and our father, God rest his soul." He speaks in Italian, his voice so achingly familiar. He sounds like our father.

"*Stronzata*." Bullshit.

"Truth." Mario touches my gun hand and eases it away from his face. Snowflakes fall into his hair making it look salt and pepper gray. Or maybe it is salt and pepper gray now. "What I tried to do was wrong. I own it. Not a day goes by I don't remember how I betrayed you." His eyes are the same color green as mine. He's stouter. Older. But otherwise, we look the same.

"I was terrified about leading the Family, and about Papà dying. I didn't feel worthy. And then when I thought you were trying to push me out—I just lost it."

Mario's two soldiers stare at their boss in shock,

clearly as surprised as I am to hear him admit any wrong-doing.

"I'm tired of seeing our ma cry on her birthday because she hasn't heard your voice in four years. I'm tired of the guilt of depriving you of Papà's last days. I have sons now—two boys—and I hate to think they would ever have bad blood between them like we have. So I'm here now. You wanna shoot me, you do it. Otherwise, I'm gonna hug you and say congratulations because you have a beautiful fucking bride."

It's a sign of my total weakness that I want to believe him. That my eyes are smarting. That my gun trembles in my hand.

I think of what Summer told me. That withholding forgiveness only harms me. On this day, when my heart is flooded with love for my bride, gratitude for my new family, it's easier to let old shit go.

Mario opens his arms, still moving slowly. Probably still not sure if I'm going to murder my own brother in front of the church on my wedding day.

I stare at him. I go by my gut on most matters, but I'm not sure I can trust myself when it comes to Mario. I want to believe him. So fucking badly.

But I'm safe. My new family flanks me. They have my back.

I nod. Tuck the gun in my waistband. Then slam a right hook into Mario's jaw.

His soldiers don't move. Al and Sonny also hold still. Like everyone knows this is the way two brothers clean their shit up.

Mario takes it. Shakes it off. Opens his arms again.

I open mine.

Thump him on the back.

"*Gesù Cristo*, you fucking guy." I'm referring less to the attempt on my life than him showing up on my wedding day.

"I hope someday you'll forgive me." Mario kisses my cheek, his own eyes wet. "I'm unarmed, so if you want to bring something down on me, do it." He spreads his arms wide once more. An invitation to have at him.

I shake my head, failing to swallow the lump in my throat.

"So, are you going to introduce me to your new family?" Mario looks pointedly at Don Al.

I swipe my eyes. "This is Don LaTorre, my father-in-law. And this is Sonny, my number one." The men shake hands, Al and Sonny putting their guns away.

"He's not allowed to move back to Sicily, so that better not be why you came here," Al informs Mario.

Mario grins. "Noted. Maybe just a honeymoon? Our ma would sure like to see his ugly face."

I draw in a deep breath of the icy air, struggling once more with my emotions. Bringing Summer home to visit Sicily would be amazing. She still complains she doesn't know me well enough. I could show her everything, until there are no secrets about my past or who I am under the tough exterior.

"Come in." I tip my head toward the church.

I lead Mario back up to the church where I just

married the only woman I ever wanted for keeps. The one who's always held my heart.

Best fucking day of my life.

And to get my brother back on the same day...fuck.

I find Summer at the door, her body and view shielded by Joey.

"It's all right," Al says.

Joey steps aside, and my beautiful bride comes out into the cold, scanning our faces with a creased brow.

I hold out my hand with a smile. "*Principessa*, this is Mario, my brother. He decided to crash our wedding."

She looks from me to my brother then steps forward and slaps Mario's face.

"Okay," he says with a surprised chuckle. "I deserve that."

Then Summer throws her arms around his neck and kisses his cheek. "Thank you for coming."

"Welcome to the family, Summer."

"Let's go inside." She looks at me. "It's time for the family photos."

I smile and tuck her against my side as we walk together back into St. Mary's.

There was a time when I thought forgiving Mario would be impossible, even if I died a miserable death. But on a day like this, with the perfect woman beside me, surrounded by my new family, it's impossible to hang onto my old grief. Mario's actions sent me here--to my new family. To Summer, my everything. And for that, I have to be grateful.

# Want Another FREE Renee Rose book?

Read Her Royal Master for free here: https://hyzr.app.
link/herroyalmaster

*Want Another FREE Renee Rose book?*

# Want More? The Gatekeeper

**The Gatekeeper**

**She's my captive.**

**My prisoner.**
**I will make her talk.**

The bratva put a gun in my hand at age thirteen. Gave me freedom, a sense of belonging, and the family I never had.

There's no way I'm going to let this slip of a woman harm my boss.

No matter how beautiful she is.

How beguiling.

How painfully fragile.

Hurting a woman, however, is not possible.

So I'll find other ways to torture her. Other, far more pleasing ways.

And in the end, my little prisoner will reveal all her secrets.

**In the end: *she will be mine*.**

# Other Titles by Renee Rose

## Made Men Series

*Don't Tease Me*

*Don't Tempt Me*

*Don't Make Me*

## Chicago Bratva

*"Prelude" in Black Light: Roulette War*

*The Director*

*The Fixer*

*"Owned" in Black Light: Roulette Rematch*

*The Enforcer*

*The Soldier*

*The Hacker*

*The Bookie*

*The Cleaner*

*The Player*

*The Gatekeeper*

## Alpha Mountain

*Hero*

*Rebel*

*Warrior*

**Vegas Underground Mafia Romance**

*King of Diamonds*

*Mafia Daddy*

*Jack of Spades*

*Ace of Hearts*

*Joker's Wild*

*His Queen of Clubs*

*Dead Man's Hand*

*Wild Card*

**Contemporary**

**Daddy Rules Series**

*Fire Daddy*

*Hollywood Daddy*

*Stepbrother Daddy*

***Master Me Series***

*Her Royal Master*

*Her Russian Master*

*Her Marine Master*

*Yes, Doctor*

***Double Doms Series***

*Theirs to Punish*

*Feral*

*Savage*

*Fierce*

*Ruthless*

## Wolf Ridge High Series

*Alpha Bully*

*Alpha Knight*

## Bad Boy Alphas Series

*Alpha's Temptation*

*Alpha's Danger*

*Alpha's Prize*

*Alpha's Challenge*

*Alpha's Obsession*

*Alpha's Desire*

*Alpha's War*

*Alpha's Mission*

*Alpha's Bane*

*Alpha's Secret*

*Alpha's Prey*

*Alpha's Sun*

### *Shifter Ops*

*Alpha's Moon*

# About Renee Rose

**USA TODAY BESTSELLING AUTHOR RENEE ROSE** loves a dominant, dirty-talking alpha hero! She's sold over two million copies of steamy romance with varying levels of kink. Her books have been featured in USA Today's *Happily Ever After* and *Popsugar*. Named Eroticon USA's Next Top Erotic Author in 2013, she has also won *Spunky and Sassy's* Favorite Sci-Fi and Anthology author, *The Romance Reviews* Best Historical Romance, and *has* hit the *USA Today* list over a dozen times with her Chicago Bratva, Bad Boy Alpha and Wolf Ranch series, as well as various anthologies.

*Renee loves to connect with readers!*
www.reneeroseromance.com
renee@reneeroseromance.com

facebook.com/reneeroseromance

twitter.com/reneeroseauthor

instagram.com/reneeroseromance

amazon.com/Renee-Rose/e/B008AS0FT0

bookbub.com/authors/renee-rose

tiktok.com/@authorreneerose

www.ingramcontent.com/pod-product-compliance
Lightning Source LLC
Chambersburg PA
CBHW020129120726
47903CB00007B/2165